PRAYER-CUSHIONS
OF THE FLESH

PRAYER-CUSHIONS OF THE FLESH

Robert Irwin

THE OVERLOOK PRESS
WOODSTOCK & NEW YORK

'The dream of monsters produces reason.'
Shaykh Ayog

This edition first published in the United States in 2002 by
The Overlook Press, Peter Mayer Publishers, Inc.
Woodstock & New York

WOODSTOCK:
One Overlook Drive
Woodstock, NY 12498
www.overlookpress.com
[for individual orders, bulk and special sales, contact our Woodstock office]

NEW YORK:
141 Wooster Street
New York, NY 10012

∞ The paper used in this book meets the requirements for paper
permanence as described in the ANSI Z39.48-1992 standard.

Library of Congress Cataloging-in-Publication Data

Irwin, Robert.
Prayer cushions of the flesh / Robert Irwin.
p. cm.
1. Sultans—Fiction. 2. Harem—Fiction. 3. Arab countries—
Fiction. 4. Middle East—Fiction. I. Title
PR6059.R96 P73 2002   823'.914—dc21   2002022875
Printed in the United States of America
ISBN 1-58567-220-3
1 3 5 7 9 8 6 4 2

CHAPTER ONE

MAN IN A CAGE

The women lay heaped like pack-ice round the walls of the Cage. As Orkhan sat shivering in the court-yard, he imagined the ladies of the Harem at ease beyond the Cage's walls. The women were braiding each others' hair; they practised embroidery; they strummed at dulcimers; they smoked narghiles; they studied books on the pleasuring of men; they scratched themselves and waited for their master. The Harem was nothing other than a series of waiting-rooms before sex. He could picture the women at their idle amusements only in his mind's eye. But sometimes – rarely – the breeze did carry the actual voices of the women, singing or laughing, over the high walls of the Cage – *the Kafes*. The rare sound of women, like the gurgling of a fountain was cooling and soothing.

He spent most of his days imagining the Harem beyond the walls. His every third thought was woman-shaped. If he had studied mathematics or astrology for a quarter of the time that he had spent thinking about women, then, young though he was, he would already have become a venerated sage. But his thoughts about women did not progress in the same way that puzzling over astrological theorems might have done. He had concluded that there was something about the smoothness of their forms which defeated logic. It seemed to Orkhan that he would have done better to have spent the last fifteen years meditating on a tiny pebble. For an inhabitant of the Cage, thinking about women was a branch of speculative philosophy, since no woman had ever set foot in the accursed place. Orkhan had last seen his mother at the age of five. He had a dim memory of being in one of the smaller pavilions in the gardens of the Palace and of vainly clinging to a vast skirt embroidered with tulips and then the black hands coming from behind to pull him away. It was all but certain that Orkhan would die before he ever saw a woman again.

The Cage was located in the heart of the warren of buildings, courtyards and covered alleys that comprised the Imperial Harem. The princes it imprisoned lived in a complex of rooms built around a flagged courtyard with a tiny garden at its centre. An arched colonnade running round two sides of the courtyard allowed the princes shelter from the sun and rain as they exercised or lazed about. A dormitory and two low-domed reception rooms led off from the colonnaded walkway and smaller cells were reached from the reception rooms. A handful of elderly deaf-mute eunuch servants shared the princes' confinement. These slept where they could in the storerooms and the kitchen on the other two sides of the courtyard. The Cage's windows all looked inwards on the dismal garden and supplies were delivered through a hole in the kitchen wall. The solitary, iron-studded door of the Cage was only opened to permit the entry of a doctor or the departure of a corpse. On the rare occasions when the door did open Orkhan and his companions strained to catch a glimpse of the corridor beyond, which was known inauspiciously as the Passage Where the Jinns Consult.

Beyond the dangerous Passage was the Harem and, beyond the Harem, the rest of the Palace and beyond the Palace was Istanbul, but Orkhan could not expand his imagination half so wide. Until a week ago there had been nine princes in the Cage. But one day last week, while the princes were lunching, picnicking in the courtyard, the door of the Cage had swung open and a pair of black eunuchs filled the opening. They did not enter the courtyard but stood at the door and beckoned to Barak, the oldest of the princes. Barak had bowed his head and passed between the eunuchs through the door and down the Passage Where the Jinns Consult. He had never looked back. Barak and Orkhan (the second oldest of the princes) had had a pact, that whichever of them should be released first, would, if he was able, send for the other. But there had been no summons from Barak nor any word of his fate. Indeed, no news of the world outside had ever entered the Cage.

The Cage was, like the Harem, a waiting room, but, whereas the Harem's odalisques waited for the delights of the bedchamber, the occupants of the Cage waited and prepared themselves for sovereignty or death. Their fates were dependent on the health and humour of the Sultan Selim and his Harem. One day it must happen that Selim would die and on that day courtiers and soldiers would come hurrying to the Cage and, having plucked out one of the princes, they would proclaim him Sultan. On the other hand, it was really more probable that, before that longed-for day arrived, Selim acting under the influence of an ominous dream or the whispered words of a jealous concubine, would suddenly and capriciously issue instructions for the execution of one or more of his sons. On that day then muscular deaf-mutes would be lining the Passage Where the Jinns Consult and one of them would be holding the silken bowstring, for it was the honourable tradition of the Ottoman house to execute its princes by strangulation.

It was possible, Orkhan thought, that Selim was dead and that Barak, who had forgotten his promise to Orkhan, was the new Sultan. It was alternatively possible that the old Sultan was still alive and had made Barak governor of Erzerum or Amasya. It was, however, all but certain that Barak was dead by strangulation. Orkhan had read that the victim of such a fate invariably experienced an erection and ejaculation, the little death of orgasm serving to mask the greater death which followed so close behind. It was one of the forms of dying classified in the books, for a reason he had not yet fathomed, as 'the Death of the Just Man'. Orkhan was as diligent in his study of death as he was in his thinking about women.

There were still hours to go before the sun would have risen above the walls of the Cage, but it had been hot all night and Orkhan was not shivering from cold. Suddenly he realised that it was not – or not just – the probable fate of Barak, which filled him with foreboding and fear. He had had a dream that night. He now remembered it, but it was not for him to interpret it, for everyone knew that, whereas the dream belonged to the person who had it, its meaning belonged to the first person it was given to for interpretation.

In search of an interpreter, Orkhan re-entered the room used by the princes as their dormitory. The seven princes lay sleeping on the stone floor. Once they had slept here on mattresses and, moreover, the reception rooms had been liberally strewn with carpets and cushions. But then Barak, their leader, had called them round him and spoken to them about the meaning of their lives. Each of them was, he said, preparing himself so as to rule as a Sultan or die like a man. So, whatever their destiny, effeminate softness had to be shunned. They should cultivate Ottoman virtues and practice to make themselves fit, hard and strong. 'Are we not men?' The princes had followed Barak's lead and from that day on they had exercised and practised at weightlifting, archery and wrestling. They bathed only in cold water. They cut their garments of silk into pieces. The princes had also gone about the Cage collecting cushions, carpets and mattresses for a bonfire. For the last two years they had slept on stone.

In the dormitory, Orkhan's half-brother, Hamid, lay staring expressionlessly up at the ceiling. He was the only one of the princes who was awake and it was he who followed Orkhan out into the courtyard. Hamid had been born to a Hungarian concubine. He

11

was red-haired and pale-skinned. His chest was remarkably hairy for one so young.

Without preamble, Orkhan began to relate his dream:

'I was in a desert in which the sand was so compact, so smooth that it was like walking on brass. The night came on and I found myself confronted and my way barred by a dark shape. It rose against me, rearing high above me, but I thrust my sword into it and it fell. Then I lay upon it using it as my pillow and waited for the dawn to come. The stars rolled swiftly over the desert and a little before the sunrise I could make out what it was that I lay upon. In shape it somewhat resembled a foetus. The smoothness of its pinkish-white bulges and curves was here and there broken up by little tufts of hair. The thing had no head, no arms and no legs, but there were fleshy flaps which might have been mouths and which seemed to pucker and breathe open as I prodded at it with my sword. Then, not knowing what to do, I left my dream.

Hamid only paused briefly before replying,

'The desert stands for continence. The sword is your sexual member. The monster is the place into which your 'sword' enters. I believe,' concluded Hamid cautiously, 'that the whole of the dream means that you will enjoy sex before sunset.'

Orkhan gave a brief, barking laugh as he gazed up at the roofs of the Cage's buildings and Hamid shrugged before suggesting a wrestling bout. The princes, as they wrestled, were accustomed to tell each other that they were building up muscle and studying at cunning. They were training to master the Empire, preparing themselves first to lead armies against Vienna and Tabriz and then to ride the ladies of the Harem, but, when Orkhan wrestled, he thought to himself that he was preparing for the terminal fight in the Passageway against the mutes with the bowstring. Orkhan and Hamid now went to the kitchen, where they would not be disturbed by the other princes. A servant sat crouched in one corner of the kitchen, but not only were the servants of the Cage deaf and mute, they were also, as far as the princes were concerned, to all intents and purposes blind and invisible as well.

The two princes stripped and oiled each other, reaching down to a jug on the floor and slapping great handfuls of olive oil onto their bodies, until they seemed to be sheathed in a body armour of gleaming leather. They lowered their heads, like a pair of angry and confronted bulls, and they wrapped their arms around each other's shoulders. They pressed hard against each other so that their oil and sweat ran together. Still locked together, they turned and turned, each trying to get a leg behind the other's. Suddenly, Orkhan stepped back and pulled Hamid to him and threw him over his extended leg. Hamid fell, but he kept his grip on Orkhan who followed him in the fall. Then Hamid was on his back slightly winded with Orkhan on top of him. His mouth formed an O of surprise, which Orkhan silenced with a kiss. Raising himself slightly, Orkhan ran his hands down Hamid's oiled cuirass of a rib-cage and muscled stomach. Pulling away yet more, he felt for Hamid's testicles and squeezed them. Hamid moaned, not from pain, but apprehension, as Orkhan, kneeling between his legs, reached for the flask of oil and, having poured more onto his left hand, he forced Hamid's legs upwards, and inserted the oil into the cleft between Hamid's buttocks. Then, as he was satisfied that the way was now prepared, he brought himself closer, so as to force his cock into the cleft of Hamid's arse. Even so, though the entry had been prepared, it was still difficult. Orkhan ground his pelvis against Hamid's body. Hamid moaned crazily. Orkhan was hammering at a door which opened only slowly. Finally he came deep inside his stepbrother.

Victory. He had used Hamid as one might use a lavatory. This was indeed part of the victory. This was the way of the warrior – a hard-fought contest where one conquered and the other played the woman's role and submitted. It had nothing to do with the love that poets and women played at. He withdrew and contemplated Hamid's hard and gleaming buttocks. He was relieved to find that he felt no desire for Hamid's body, for desire of the flesh made one vulnerable, womanish. Victory, yet it was, he knew, only a shadow victory, as sex with a man was reported to be only an adumbration of sex with a woman. It was only a game, an exercise, practice for the real war which was between men and women. On the other hand, it was better than being in bed with a eunuch. As those who have had sex with eunuchs will know, eunuchs are childish, petulant creatures. They are always demanding chocolates or toys for their favours.

Orkhan lay beside Hamid, looking up at the ceiling and thinking of the day which stretched ahead. It would be precisely the same day as yesterday – only it would bear a different date. They were all schooled in boredom. The same day came round again and again and in it they wrestled and engaged in target practice. Some of the princes gardened, measuring out their days against the slow growth of plants. Others raced cockroaches, placed bets on the fall of leaves in the wind, or sat like idiots watching the sunlight climbing up a wall. Orkhan read books on miscellaneous topics – the manners and customs of the inhabitants of the Russian steppes, sex-lives of the eunuchs, how to cook edible clays, conjuring tricks with eggs – whatever literature was procurable through the hole in the wall. Sometimes, he wrote poems or love-letters to the Ladies of the Harem and, having scrolled them round the shafts of arrows, he fired them over the enclosing roofs of the Cage. No arrows ever came back. Now he lay back beside Hamid and poured more oil over his cock which was sore. Hamid, seeing what he was doing, crawled over to suck the cock, working his tongue from the base to the tip until Orkhan came again, this time in Hamid's mouth. At length, bored with each other's company, they went next door to the tiny bath-house to wash the oil off.

Hamid limped off back to the dormitory. Orkhan was left alone in the courtyard – apart from a couple of old deaf-mutes that is. He felt his sense of triumph ebb away, for he now asked himself was it to him that Hamid had submitted, or was it to the dream? Destiny, after all, has its own power. Suddenly the wind changed and the women's voices could be heard. It seemed to him that they sounded unusually excited, like the twittering of exotic birds disturbed by the proximity of a predator. Then the door of the Cage opened. A black hand beckoned and Orkhan walked towards it.

CHAPTER TWO

THE PERFUMED BATTLEFIELD

He walked in front of the mutes down the Passage Where the Jinn Consult and stumbled slightly on the uneven flagstones. High bottle-glass windows let in a greenish light. Orkhan's eyes drank in the details of unfamiliar stonework. As he walked, he kept his arms tense against his sides, for he was waiting for the descent of the bowstring. Yet nothing happened and he kept walking. It seemed that the invisible Jinns who consulted in this corridor had decided on life for Orkhan.

At the end of the passage stood a tiny man.

'Hail, Sultan Orkhan, Lord of the Empire in the East and in the West. Greetings to my new master, raised from the dead and born again. Squinting my eyes in astonishment, I behold the earthy clods fall away from your body as your august mother, the Valide Sultan, confers on you the shining robe of a second life. Then accept her gift and follow me.'

As the dwarf turned to lead the way, Orkhan saw that the strange little man was also humpbacked. He followed the dwarf out of the passageway and, taken aback at finding himself in such a vast open space, he reeled. Though at first his eyes could not comprehend what it was that they gazed upon, he soon came to understand that he was walking in a large garden.

He reached forward and spun the dwarf round,

'Who are you?'

'I am your Vizier for as long as I can behold my shadow in the sunshine of your favour, but God knows that, whatever the angle of the sun, the shadow that a body like mine can cast must always be a short one.'

'How am I Sultan? Is Selim dead? What has happened to Barak?'

'Alas for the Sultan Selim. Indeed the parrot of his great spirit, breaking the bonds of its sensual cage is obliged to set out for the eternal city.'

'You mean that my father is dead?'

'Even a Sultan must one day step off from the world of being into the abyss of non-existence.'

'Where is Barak?'

'You will shortly behold him face to face.'

'Why have I been freed?'

The Vizier responded impatiently,

'Who has said that you were free? You are not free. The Sultan is the least free of all mortals, being burdened with the cares of justice and government. The good sultan will always be a slave to his subjects.'

Now the impatient vizier turned and broke into a trot, heading towards a pavilion made of porcelain in the centre of the garden. Orkhan's brains boiled with unanswered questions, but there was no time to ask them before he followed the dwarf through the door.

A baby gazelle was skittering across the porcelain floor, its legs splaying out as the little creature was unable to find any hold on such a smooth surface. Servant girls knelt around the gazelle trying to catch and calm it. A raddled, older woman sprawled back

20

on a cushioned bench at the far end, laughing at the unavailing efforts of her servants. Orkhan found that he did after all remember her.

'Mother, don't you recognise me?'

The Valide Sultan nodded and waved her hands apologetically, yet she could not stop laughing. This was the woman who had let him be taken off to prison and left him to languish there for fifteen years. At last, one of the servant girls caught the gazelle, scooped it up and carried it out of the pavilion. Now the Valide Sultan's eyes came to rest on Orkhan. Indeed, all the women in the pavilion were slyly watching him from beneath darkened lashes. No one said anything. He for his part stood transfixed, looking at the women. They were not like the women in the picture books he and his brothers used to study in the Cage. The ones in miniature paintings were slender, stick-like figures who gazed out expressionlessly from the pictures. But the real women in the pavilion were heavy, fleshy creatures, who, despite their size, did not seem to have quite outgrown the shapes of babyhood. Orkhan, seeing women for the first time in so many years, experienced pity for them, since all that softness, those fragile wrists, pendulous breasts and heavy bottoms ill-equipped such creatures for survival in a man's world.

At length, remembering himself and guessing at imperial etiquette, Orkhan bowed to his mother. He came closer to seek her embrace. As he did so, she raised herself from the cushions and placed a finger on his lips.

'You have been a long time in the Cage. Even so,

explanations can wait. After fifteen years in the Cage, you must be impatient for a girl.' She put on an expression of mock solemnity. 'Very impatient . . . The Vizier will find you one.'

And she waved her hand in dismissal.

Outside in the garden, Orkhan told his Vizier that the girl could wait. The first thing he had to do was summon a council of ministers.

The Vizier, however, disagreed,

'You are master of the Empire from the Euphrates to the Danube and there is certainly much to do, but first you must be master of your Harem, for a man who cannot master his Harem cannot master himself, still less an empire. Besides you need an heir as soon as possible. Now, would you like an ugly concubine or a beautiful one?'

'What? Why would I choose an ugly one?'

'Well, they say beauty fades, but that ugliness is eternal. Are you sure you would not prefer an ugly concubine?'

'I am quite sure. Bring me a beautiful girl.'

'Aha! You remember that earlier in the garden I told you that you were not free? Now you must see the truth of my words, for you must admit that you are not free, for you are not free to prefer ugliness over beauty. Aha! Caught you there!'

'I see that I have much to learn,' replied Orkhan carefully, thinking as he did so that on the following morning he would dismiss his Vizier. 'Now, find me a beautiful girl. Let us get this over with quickly.'

'I think I have a good girl for you on your first day. She is a Georgian. Since your Empire is at war with

Georgia, she will be good training for you. Learning to ride her is like learning how to conquer Georgia. She will be the horse that will take you into the heart of their lands. Oh! One last thing. Do everything you please with her, except that, whatever you do, on no account should you let the viper drink at the Tavern of the Perfume-Makers.'

After washing and perfuming himself, Orkhan was conducted into a tiny rib-vaulted cell, which was richly hung with velvet embroideries, but yet not so different from the rooms he had been familiar with in the Cage. On the far side of the cell was a raised marble platform. On this platform was a bed and at the foot of the bed there was a lectern which supported a large open book. The place seemed surprisingly cold. Then, as he walked towards the platform, Orkhan looked down and saw that he trod on ice. The bed and the velvet hangings notwithstanding, the place was really just a cellar for the storage of ice. Mystified, Orkhan carefully made his way to the bed and waited. In the Cage he had read about the ice-pits of the sultans and how ice in great blocks was brought by racing camels from Mount Olympus and then packed down and stored in deep pits within the palace – all this merely so that the sultans could enjoy iced drinks throughout the summer. But why should he be here?

Orkhan had not waited long before he saw the door open and something come slithering across the ice towards him. In the half-light it might have been a dog or a jinn. Then the thing raised its head, and he saw that it, or rather, she was a woman who was dragging herself towards him. Her heavy earrings and bracelets jingled as she did so. She knelt on the edge of the marble and kissed his feet, before raising her face to him.

'I am Anadil,' she said.

She had large eyes and dark curls peeped out from an intricately-made cap of gold and silver filigree.

'It is a pretty name,' she continued. 'Do you not think so? It means "Nightingales".'

Orkhan tried gently to pull her up to his level, but she resisted.

'Tell me first that my name is pretty.' She was pouting.

'Your name is pretty. Now come and sit beside me.'

Reluctantly she joined him on the bed. Again, Orkhan made to pull her towards him. Even though she was not strong enough to resist him, she still protested,

'Not so fast! You are like a beast from the depths of the forest. I am not to be treated in this way.'

'I treat you how I like. I am your Sultan.'

And Orkhan pressed himself against her, his swelling member against her thigh. He wanted to bury himself in Anadil. His hands moved over her body, seeking a way to strip her of her costume, but she looked sulky and kept shifting under his hands and, though her yellow silken robe with its unfamiliar hooks and catches, was flimsy enough for him to have ripped it off her, she was additionally protected by what amounted to jewelled armour. A girdle of pierced coins and amulets encircled her waist and heavy, many-layered necklaces hung over her breasts.

'Slow down! It is as if you had never seen a woman before.' Then she tittered as she realised what she had said. 'But, of course, in the Cage there are no women! A body like mine is unfamiliar territory to such a one as you ... Even so, if you have waited fifteen years for me, a few more hours' dalliance is but a little thing. You have to please me.'

'No, you have to please me. I am your Sultan,' Orkhan insisted once more.

'It is the other way around. Otherwise I will be unhappy and I will make you unhappy. It is no disgrace for a sultan to submit himself to a concubine, if he desires her, for that is the way of courtly love. In any case, I can see that I please you already,' pointing to the swelling between his legs. 'What have you got down there? It is very big, is it not? Is it not big because it likes me?'

Orkhan nodded.

'I am pleased that it likes me. Does the rest of you like me?'

He nodded. Though her childish catechism exasperated him almost beyond endurance, the smell of Anadil, intimate and bitter, was working on him like a spell of subjugation, so that whatever she wanted, she could have, if only he could have her.

'Well, smile then – and you will have to learn to talk properly and not just shake your head. I think I will have to teach you how you must speak to a concubine. You are so innocent – just a boy really. But there is no need to be frightened of me. All you have to do is tell me that I am pretty and which parts of me are especially pretty.'

25

'You are the most beautiful women I have ever seen'. This was no great concession on Orkhan's part. As he contemplated her, he was struck by the delicate colouring of her face and the soft vulnerability of her arms. If only the catechism could be over, then he might be in full possession of this softly, enchanting curvy creature. Although she was telling him not to be frightened, he still sensed something frightening in the supernatural quality of Anadil's beauty, which was like the beginning of terror. She seemed to him to be a visitant from another world.

'Well, that will do to begin with. Now, if you take your hands off me, I will undress myself for you.'

Stepping away from the bed, she stood to let cascades of gold, silver and brass drop to the marble platform, followed by her yellow robe. In a few moments she stood naked before him. Then she turned away, and looking over her shoulder, she said,

'In the Harem, we girls like to read before we go to bed.'

She went over to the lectern and came back to the bed bearing the book. She sat close beside Orkhan and spread the book between her thighs.

'It is called '*The Perfumed Battlefield: or Questions Posed by the White Sultan to the Dark Girl,*' she said, spelling out the words with difficulty.

She turned the pages. The book was illustrated. Together they contemplated exquisite little pictures of women surrounded by ditches and ramparts, men advancing with battering rams and long, hooked implements, and brightly coloured smokes drifting across fields strewn with flowers and corpses. In flimsy looking castles men and women encountered one another in hand-to-hand combat. There were also abstract diagrams painted in gold and black with arrows of direction and schematic flags. On the last page was the image of a man, painted all gold. A woman knelt in front of him, her face pressed to his groin, and another stood behind him, peeping over his shoulder, and he was grinning madly – a silvery gleam in a golden face. Having reached this image, Anadil hastily riffled backwards through the pages.

'Here,' said Anadil, leaning heavily against Orkhan, is "The Chapter on the Need for Good Intelligence" and this is "The Section on the Naming of Parts".

One hand moved across the page, marking her place as she read. She was stroking her breasts with her other hand.

'What are these called?'

'They are called breasts,' replied Orkhan, unable to keep the irritation out of his voice.

To his astonishment, she slapped him lightly on the face.

'Only the vulgar call them that. These are my moons. It is the language of love and poetry. Look here, it says so in the book. You have to practise. Say to me, I love your full moons.'

And she offered them up to be kissed.

Now, since she was now sliding a hand underneath his robe and fumbling between his legs, there was no power in Orkhan to refuse. Even if he thought that her games were silly, she could be indulged for a few moments more. He was prepared to crawl over the ice, bark like a dog and sit up to beg if only she would grant him what he desired. Her breasts were soft and came to delicate points.

'I love your full moons,' he repeated obediently and kissed them.

'And what is this between your legs?'

'It is my cock.'

She brought her hand up from between his legs to slap him again.

'That is very vulgar. I would be ashamed to call it that. In the Harem we call it the pigeon, or, sometimes, the one-eyed man, or sometimes the cherry-blossom branch, or again the weeping one. It has many names. Here they are in the book.'

Then she let the book drop to the floor and, leaning over him, she delicately forced her tongue between his lips. At the end of the kiss, she drew back a little and sticking out her tongue again, she pointed to it.

'What do we call this?'

'I do not know and I do not care.'

'We call this the coral branch, or the viper, or the honey-spoon. But I can see that you are impatient to begin. So just one last lesson, just one more word to memorise.' She threw herself back on the bed and pointed between her legs. 'Would you like to know what this is called?'

'People who are not poets call it the cunt,' said Orkhan.

'Oh, we have a prettier name for it than that. It is the Tavern of the Perfume-Makers. Come close to examine it carefully please.'

Surely this lesson, this inspection, was absurd. But Orkhan thought that there would be no real harm in indulging the girl's whims for now. Even if her chatter was tiresome, her body was certainly desirable. Her face was like a glorious promise of nobility and intelligence, yet her prattle was sheer childishness. How was it possible for anyone to be simultaneously so beautiful and so silly? Well, he would indulge her for now. But then, to ensure that no one else in the Harem should hear of the humiliations she had put him through, he would have her executed on the following morning. As he lowered his face between her thighs, he pictured himself watching her execution on the morrow. He would give the mutes instructions for her slow impalement. Unaware of the madness in his head, Anadil sighed and spread her legs a little further.

'Does the sight please you?' she enquired coyly.

'It pleases me very much,' and he might have said more, but she pulled his face closer yet and Orkhan found himself tasting her. The flavour was unfamiliar, bitter, strangely seductive.

'Now we are ready,' she sighed and she was indeed moist between the legs.

But no sooner had Orkhan thrown off his robe than she sprang away.

'Yes, yes, we are ready. But not here. Down there,' she said pointing to the surface of the ice pit.

Anadil stepped down from the marble platform and, wincing slightly, lay back upon the ice.

'Come back, Anadil. Not on the ice. What is wrong with the bed. Come back here!'

'It is better on the ice. That is why we are here. The coldness delays the climax and increases the pleasure.' She wriggled seductively. 'Come on lover.'

'This is madness!'

Anadil looked up at him sulky and disappointed.

'We Harem girls heard that all you princes in the Cage were men of stone, ready for anything and invulnerable to cold, hunger or pain. But now a little girl like me can lie on the ice and you dare not.'

'It is madness,' Orkhan repeated stupidly.

'Come on, don't be boring. It is more fun on the ice. Besides I will be beneath you as your prayer-cushion or above you as your blanket. But don't let me get cold here alone.' She reached up her arms to him in supplication.

Orkhan could feel a fire melting his insides. He had to have her. He descended to the ice and she fingered his torso appreciatively before wrapping herself around him. Then she reached down for his branch of plum blossom, or whatever it was she had called it, and guided it between her legs. Although, even before entering Anadil, Orkhan had thought that he was on the very edge of exploding from desire, it was as she had predicted; the ice delayed the climax as their bodies could get no purchase on its surface and she slithered about under him. Droplets of water covered both their bodies. As he kept moving inside her, he thought he glimpsed something dark and motionless in the depths of the ice below. A big fish, or just a shadow in the mind. It was a strange kind of race, he thought, between the heat of his desire and

30

the freezing chill of their strange bed. The fun and mischief had now gone out of Anadil's face. Her legs were now locked round his back and she was crying in frustration as he thrust within her. He, for his part, felt himself so desperate to come to a climax within this strange creature, that he was by now ready to offer up himself for slow impalement on the morrow, if only he could have what he wanted now. Nothing else mattered. Now. Finally he came in a hot thick torrent.

'Oh, my Sultan!'

They lay together briefly collapsed in each others' arms. Then Anadil wriggled impatiently under him.

'Now my bottom is cold. You can warm it for me.'

And slipping out from under him, she rolled over in the melting slush. He ran his hands over her wet rump and smoothed away tiny particles of ice.

'That will not warm my bottom. You can spank it, if you like.'

He pulled himself up on his elbows and, as he contemplated her soft little bottom, he felt desire stirring within him again. But, suddenly, even before Orkhan could raise his hand to deliver the first slap, she uttered a brief cry. Then she looked over her shoulder at Orkhan. Her face was grim and her teeth were chattering so much that she was impossible to understand at first. Finally Orkhan heard her say,

'There is a face in the ice! We have been making love upon someone's tomb! Look at it! You have to look!'

31

Peering over Anadil's shoulder, Orkhan could now with difficulty just make out the body through the still thick layers of ice. He saw Barak grinning fiercely up at him.

CHAPTER THREE

THE FAT BUTTERFLY

Outside in the corridor, a pair of mutes barred their way. A third, seeing them emerge from the ice-cell, disappeared back down the corridor. In a little while, he returned with the Vizier. The Vizier started talking before Orkhan could open his mouth.

'Now, you have beheld your brother face to face, just as was promised. In this place promises are always kept. Alas, that they are almost never kept in the way one is expecting. Yet the showing of your brother was meant kindly.'

'Kindly!'

'Yes it was meant to be a clear and vivid warning for you. I think that it is like the rearing of lion cubs. As everyone knows, the cubs are always born dead, but the loving lioness tends them and licks them into shape and after a few days they are made alive. Even so, it sometimes happens that there is a cub which cannot be licked into shape.'

'You mean that it was the Valide Sultan who had my brother killed?'

'A mother kill her own son! And she is your mother too! How could you think such a thing of your own mother?' The Vizier did indeed seem genuinely shocked. However he continued, 'Even so, it is always rewarding to contemplate the ways of the

35

animal kingdom. The beasts of the desert and jungle have much to teach the politic man.'

'But what have you to teach me? Who did kill Barak?'

'Wild surmise will infallibly miss its mark. Barak was like a man making his way along a precipitous mountain ledge in a snow storm. Then he looked down and, having looked down, he lost his nerve and, having lost his nerve, he lost his footing and with it his life. It is best to think of your brother as an unlucky mountain man. Alternatively, you may think of your brother as a man seated at his ease and feasting at a party. Then Death the Butler comes round with a bitter cup. Your brother seizes the cup and drinks deeply from it. Yes, perhaps that is better – to think of your brother as a man leaving a party.'

Suddenly Orkhan thought of Anadil. He did not want her reporting on what had taken place in the ice-cell, or, for that matter on the conversation he was now having with the Vizier. He turned towards her, intending to have her placed under immediate arrest, but she was no longer anywhere to be seen. He turned back to the Vizier,

'That girl, Anadil, who was with me, I want her placed under close confinement under the guard of deaf mutes.'

'I shall lose no time in carrying out your command, O Sultan,' said the Vizier, looking thoughtful. 'So, she did not please you? I did think that you would have been better off with an ugly woman. The thing about ugly women is that it takes longer to achieve . . . '

'Tell me some other time! Your next task is to summon the ministers to an immediate meeting.'

'I will lose no time in dealing with this also. The ministers long to bask in the radiance of your newly risen sun. But they are dispersed throughout the city and it will take time to have them fetched and, besides, you must be hungry. Yes, surely it is time to eat, for you have not eaten since you came out of the Cage. I will arrange for food to be brought to you.'

'See to it then, and the summoning of the ministers and the arrest of the girl. I must be busy. I am impatient.'

'Yes, you are like your brother.'

Then the Vizier led him to another small room. Most of the floor was covered in cushions in the midst of which there was a low table. Having ushered him in, the Vizier was about to hurry away, but an afterthought struck him,

'One last thing, you did not, by any chance, let the viper drink at the Tavern of the Perfume-Makers?'

'Certainly not,' lied Orkhan impatiently. 'I have no idea what you are talking about.'

'All may still be well then,' said the Vizier.

A few moments later, mutes appeared, bearing vast silver trays covered with snacks. Orkhan ate and dozed. Then he was being shaken awake. The Vizier was bending anxiously over him.

'The Valide Sultan wants to see you. I will come with you and wait for you, so that I can conduct you from her august majesty's presence to the audience chamber where the council of ministers will meet'.

Once again they made their way across the garden

to the porcelain pavilion. This time Orkhan found it impossible to advance more than a couple of steps beyond its door. A great carpet – the Carpet of Mirth – now covered most of the porcelain floor of the pavilion and a writhing mound of shrieking and giggling young women tumbled across it, displaying, as they did so, parts of their bodies which should not be seen in public. At every moment more women, having taken their turn at casting the dice, threw themselves upon the heap. The fall of the dice determined where, on which squares, they should place their hands and feet. From the bottom of the heap of writhing bodies, voices could be heard vainly pleading to be let out to throw the dice again and improve on their position.

At the far end of the room the Valide Sultan looked on with indulgence. Seeing Orkhan, she pointed to the heap of women in between them and said,

'Would you like to join them, Orkhan?'

He shook his head vigorously.

'But there is a playmate of yours somewhere in there, I think.'

In answer to these words, Anadil's triumphant head emerged from the shifting mass of robes and limbs. Though she smiled brightly up at him, he looked on Anadil and her companions who sported on the Carpet of Mirth with revulsion. He was thinking of Barak suspended in the ice.

The Valide Sultan seemed perfectly oblivious to Orkhan's hostility. She lolled back comfortably on the cushions and smiled lazily. She had to raise her voice above the squeaks and giggles of the young women,

'Poor Anadil has not had much luck on the Carpet this afternoon. But I hear she had better fortune in her games with you this morning. I hear you two had a little wrestle – and she trapped your head in a leg-lock. That counts the same as a fall in wrestling, does it not? So what shall be her prize?'

Orkhan wanted to say that Anadil deserved nothing less than arrest and impalement, but in the situation he now found himself in, faced by the Valide Sultan and this horde of laughing women, such a thing seemed all but impossible to say. He hesitated. Then, he reflected that he was, after all, the Sultan. So he took a deep breath and said it,

'She deserves nothing less than death. Anadil will be arrested and these follies are now at an end.'

There were cries of dismay from the floor.

'So no one may laugh and Anadil must die, in order that you can keep your miserable self-pride!' the Valide Sultan cried out. She was not smiling now. 'A beautiful woman in her youth is to be slain to protect my prince's sulks!'

Orkhan did not trouble to reply. He hurried out of the door and angrily confronted the Vizier who was waiting anxiously.

'Wretched slave, I thought I had told you to arrest Anadil.'

'Alas, my Sultan, I am indeed a wretched slave, for I have had the eunuchs search high and low for her, but they have not been able to find her.'

'She has been in the pavilion playing silly games

with the other concubines. Arrest her now – and I want the Valide Sultan escorted to her chambers and placed under close confinement. She is to communicate with no one.'

'I will lose no time in carrying out your commands. I go like an arrow shot from your bowstring. I become the words of your commands floating on the breath of your will, for the fulfilment of your will is the height of all our desires. Would you like to proceed to the council chamber now?'

The Vizier tugged at Orkhan's sleeve. As they walked away from the porcelain pavilion, the Vizier continued to speak in a low mutter – as if he were speaking to himself,

'There are gates which should never be entered. There are certain keys for which there are no locks. There are hidden places within the women's quarters which are not safe for a man. There are certain passageways into which a man should not stick his nose. This palace has doors which can take a man out of this world . . . But you tell me that the viper has not entered the Tavern. That at least is good.'

'Speak plainly or keep silent,' Orkhan commanded.

The Vizier looked hard at Orkhan.

'Well, I see that I will have to be plain with you. You must understand that the festering idleness of the Harem girls engenders wicked thoughts, so that they do all sorts of things that they should not. Flowers of evil grow in a bed of boredom. One of the concubines' wickedest tricks is that they smear an addictive paste between their thighs, so that a man having put his face where he should not and having tasted the drugged potion which is on offer at the Tavern of the Perfume-Makers, soon becomes addicted. That man will end up begging for more, kneeling before them with his tongue hanging out. Nothing will seem more important to him than to be allowed to have another taste. So the girls of the Harem can turn their master into their slave. It is all part of this abominable Prayer-Cushion business.'

'What Prayer-Cushion business?'

'Ah, here we are at the council chamber! The ministers will surely be coming along shortly. As your Vizier, I advise you to ask not about what concerns you not, lest you hear what pleases you not.'

The council chamber turned out to be a spacious wooden kiosk on a low hill in the Palace's garden. Its interior was painted with scenes of hunting, picnicking and flirtation. Though pleasant, the place hardly seemed suitable for the transaction of government business. The Vizier, possibly anxious not to be interrogated further about any prayer-cushions, having made a hasty obeisance, hurried away. Orkhan seated himself on one of the low, cushioned benches in the kiosk and waited.

He had not waited long before someone entered. It was not a minister, but a woman, who came wriggling on her belly across the floor, making her way towards him. This time it was not Anadil, for the waggling rump, sheathed in a tight black robe belonged to an older and bulkier woman. She did not raise her head or say anything, but once she had reached the bench on which he was sitting, she set to work, licking his feet and sucking at his toes.

41

Occasionally she moaned, whether from pleasure or disgust was not clear.

Orkhan was so surprised that for a while he allowed her to have her way with his feet before he recollected himself and pulled them away.

'Go away, you foolish woman!' he told her. 'I am not in the mood for your Harem games. This is a place for business, not pleasure. Get out before the ministers arrive.'

'But, oh my master, I am here on business. I am the first of the Sultan's petitioners. I prostrate myself utterly before you, for I have come to beg for mercy for my mistress, Anadil. My name is Perizade, which means the Fairy-Born.'

And only now did she raise her head. Orkhan found himself gazing on a tear-stained, pudgy face. Perizade's nose was slightly hooked and her lips were thick. Her heavy breasts pressed tight against the black sheath. As Orkhan gazed on them, she too looked down on them and smiled.

'I abase myself utterly. I am yours to do with as you please. I am the Sultan's prayer-cushion. Do with me as you will. Please forgive Anadil. Unless you forgive my mistress, she will be angry with me.'

'You are mistaken. She will be dead rather than angry.'

Perizade thought about this. But she looked unconvinced,

'But you must give mercy to Anadil.'

'"Must" is not a word to be used to sultans. Anadil is my slave and I shall deal with her as I choose.'

42

'It is true that Anadil is your slave, but she is a slave of her body first. It is the same with all of us. From the moment of our birth we, all of us, find ourselves swimming in a great ocean of desire, whose sexual tides carry us to unfamiliar shores, whether we will or no.'

Orkhan snorted at her words, but Perizade continued,

'It is certain that none of us are free. We are all driven by Destiny. Destiny is a mad scribe, who writes our stories on our bodies. It writes upon our skins, covering them with a script of lines, spots, veins, freckles, and swellings.'

'So, Perizade, you are a philosopher?' Orkhan was amused in spite of himself.

'I am a washerwoman, Oh Sultan. I wash the clothes of Anadil and the other concubines. She is young and you are young. If she was foolish last night, it was only a child's game and that was perhaps the only fun she will ever have. You are a sultan and we are your slaves, but we are all humans as well. Anadil is not a toy to be torn apart and discarded when she does not please you. Think again. Spare my mistress and I will grant you anything you desire.'

' How can you, a washerwoman to slaves, give the Sultan anything he does not already have?'

'I can give you good fortune.'

'What? You are a lucky slave or something?'

'Or something. I tell fortunes. I am a phallomancer.' She licked her lips in a suggestive fashion and continued,

'Show me your cock and I will tell you your

43

fortune,' and, rising from her kneeling posture, she stood over Orkhan, so that her breasts hung over his face and she tugged urgently at his robe. Orkhan, who was curious about his fortune, did not resist. Having uncovered his cock, which stiffened instantly, she set to licking it.

'This helps to bring the veins out,' she explained, before reapplying her mouth to its divinatory work.

Her mouth worked its way from base to tip. She gave the tip a special tongue-lashing. Then, holding the swollen cock between thumb and forefinger, she drew back to contemplate her work.

'Sultan or shop-keeper, they are all pretty much alike at first sight. There are just tiny differences in the veins for the fortune-teller to work with.' She ran a tracking finger down his cock. 'This line, for example, is your heart line, and over here your line of procreation . . . Taste is also part of it,' she confided. 'I should say that you are a kind man, only you have not had enough tenderness. Ah, that is unusual! Your line of Destiny crosses both the line of Mars and the girdle of Venus. How interesting!'

'What does that mean?'

' I am getting wet thinking about it. It means that you will fall in love and marry and, if I have read these lines correctly, our fates and our sexual juices will mingle, for I am the lucky woman you will marry and make your queen!'

Orkhan emitted a barking laugh.

'No it is true,' she insisted. 'Your fortune follows the mouth of the fortune-teller. But, if you do not believe me, you can see for yourself. Just as Destiny has written upon your cock, so will my fate be written on my cunt. The science of vulvascopy is very ancient. Is it not said that round the cunt of every woman is written the names of the men who are destined to enter it? Come on, come and have a good look!' she urged, as she wriggled about.

With some difficulty she pulled the dress up over her hips. Then she lay back upon the cushions and spread her legs. Intrigued despite himself, he lowered his face between her plump thighs.

'My fortune will be written on the folds closest to the clitoris. Hurry up and tell me, am I not going to be your queen?' Her voice, no longer that of wheedling petitioner, had turned imperious.

Unlike Anadil, Perizade was not clean shaven between the legs. Orkhan gazed at the folds of the vulva, uncertain what it was that he was looking for. The fancy entered his head that he was gazing on an oracular mouth. It seemed to him to be whispering indistinctly, summoning him to approach closer. Almost swooning, he did find himself moving in closer. He thought that it was as if the strange mouth did indeed have the power to command him. Then, at the very last moment, he remembered the Vizier's warning about not letting the viper sup at the Tavern of the Perfume-Makers and he pulled away.

'What did you do that for, you silly man?' Perizade's voice was shrill. 'I want to know my fortune. But I know I'm destined to be your queen.'

Orkhan made no reply, but knelt and gazed at Perizade's breasts and hips. His memory of Anadil was of a girl whose flesh was young and healthy, yet in a sense devoid of life. But Perizade's soft heavy body was different. It seemed to speak to him of lived experience – of so many meals eaten, carpets sat upon, men embraced – and, because of this, it was infinitely desirable. He had to have her now, no matter how much he might regret it later. (He was quite certain that he would regret it.) Once again he moved towards her and placed a hand on one of her thighs.

'What are you doing?' She tried ineffectively to pull the dress back down over her hips.

'I want you, Perizade.'

'This is not what was meant to happen!'

'This is your destiny,' replied Orkhan.

It was after all the one-eyed man and not the viper who forced his way through the door of the Tavern of the Perfume-Makers. He pressed down hard upon the washerwoman, not caring how he hurt her. She was stony-faced and sweaty. She made no moves to help him, but her body quivered under his thrusts like a mattress filled with water. Perizade was silently weeping. She did not want to submit, but in the end she did and, at the last moment, she put her arms around him and hugged him tightly.

Orkhan lay for a long time on top of her, kissing and licking the tears from her cheeks. When, finally he did withdraw and rolled over to lie beside her, he fell instantly into a heavy post-coital doze. He awoke to a kind of nightmare, in which some immovable weight, some monstrous creature perhaps, was squatting on his face, so that he was unable to breathe. Then he realised that this was no dream, but that Perizade was indeed sitting on his face. He could dimly hear her crooning with pleasure. In a thrice, he threw her off and pushed her onto the floor. But, though he had swiftly dealt with the incubus, it was not before the viper, possessed of a will of its own, had once again drunk in the Tavern of the Perfume-Makers.

With her dress still hitched up above her hips, Perizade knelt at his feet once more, but she was smug in her prostration,

'Now that you have acquired a taste for me I know that you will forgive Anadil and make me your queen.'

'Witch! You are mistaken. You will share her fate.' And pulling his robe around him, Orkhan rushed out of the pavilion.

CHAPTER FOUR

PARROT IN A CAGE

The sky was by now an inky blue and continued to darken. A mute who stood outside the door of the pavilion, seeing Orkhan emerge, pointed towards a path, indicating that he should follow it. The shingled path was lined on both sides by a series of lacquer and silk screens topped by flambeaux. As he walked, the wailing of Perizade grew faint behind him and he began to hear the sound of running water and, further away, women's voices and the beating of a tambourine. It was cooler now and the arrival of evening, released unfamiliar perfumes. Orkhan walked slowly, alert to every sound and movement, for he now sensed that the paradise he walked in was a poisoned one. At last, he came out from between the screens into a large circular space framed by chenars and cypresses. At the centre was a dried-up fountain and on its sculpted edge sat a stunted figure.

Orkhan addressed the Vizier peremptorily,

'Arrest that wretched woman in the pavilion. I do not want to see her again — or anyone like her.'

'To serve the Sultan is all our joy,' replied the Vizier, but he did not move.

Orkhan looked sharply at the Vizier,

'And where are the ministers? Should not some of them be here by now?'

'Some of the ministers were indeed here before

51

now, oh my master, but, since you were entertaining that woman, it seemed inappropriate to admit them to your presence, so I sent them tiptoeing away. They are, of course, greatly looking forward to transacting government business on some future occasion. But Perizade did not please you? We can easily find another woman. My wife is a hunchback like me. I could lend her to you. You would find her a challenge, I am . . . '

Orkhan gestured him to be quiet. They gazed at one another. Then, after a long silence, Orkhan spoke,

'No ministers have been here really, have they?'

'No.'

'And no ministers are coming, are they – ever?'

'No.'

'And you have not arrested Anadil?'

'No.'

'And you will not arrest Perizade either?'

'No,' the Vizier was looking a little uncomfortable. 'I am the Sultan's slave and I hoped for the best, so I did not want him to hear what would have displeased him.'

'Well then, you have failed, for I am most displeased. You are no longer my Vizier. Before I have you arrested, you will explain yourself.' But, even as he heard himself speak, Orkhan knew that his words were empty and the Vizier now turned scornful,

'You cannot arrest me! I think that you must be living in some blood-boltered dream of your own, going around giving orders: "Arrest this person!", "Arrest that person!" "Execute this person!". The world you find yourself in is not like that, nor is it in your powers to dismiss me as Vizier.'

Orkhan sat down heavily beside the Vizier.

'So, tell me what is the world really like? I think it is time for you to tell me what will please me not.'

'Oh my master, you may think that you rule as Sultan over an empire of men . . . but here in the Harem, you actually live on sufferance in a republic of women. There was a time – a hundred years ago perhaps – when the Sultan ruled over the Harem and the Palace, as he did over the Empire. Then the *fitna* of the women occurred. You should know about this word, *fitna*. It has entered our language from the Arabic. It means discord, revolution, sedition, but it also means temptation or seduction. It has other meanings too. It means a trial, burning, and melting, rapture, madness and possession. Finally, *fitna* also means woman. A hundred years ago, women used their seductive powers to stage a revolution in the Palace and they used beguilement, artifice and drugs to enslave the man who was then Sultan. Ever since that time, the woman who holds the rank of Valide Sultan has controlled everything. The eunuchs, the mutes and the slave girls all move to her command – and only her command.'

'So I – so the Sultan has become nothing but a plaything of the Harem?'

'Alas! Would that it might be so! It is easy, after all, to imagine worse fates than that. No, things in the Harem have taken a graver turn. It is all because of the hellish Prayer-Cushion movement . . . '

'What is this business with prayer-cushions?'

53

'Ask not. It is better that you know nothing of this – at least until you absolutely have to.'

'No, the time for secrets and whispers is over. I want to know everything now. Speak plainly and tell me what danger can there possibly be in prayer-cushions?'

'Well, if you must . . . but you will be sorry that you asked. Of course there is no danger in a cushion, in the sense of some soft, embroidered pad on which a man may take his ease. But I speak of the movement known as the Prayer-Cushions of the Flesh. It is a very ancient and evil sect followed by some of the tribes who inhabit the depths of the forests and swamps of the Balkans. Though it has flourished in the Balkans, it has nothing to do with either Islam or Christianity, being much older than either. Its devotees hold that man can only reach God through women. They believe that women are not of the same race as men. Women are spirits, friendly demons of a kind, who have been given flesh and placed upon the Earth in order to monitor man's spiritual progress towards the Divinity. Women are men's prayer-cushions and intercourse with them prepares man for Mystical Union with the Divinity.'

Orkhan pondered the Vizier's words, before asking,

'Indeed, it all seems strange and mad, but it does not seem so very dangerous. Why should any man fear the Prayer-Cushion of the Flesh?'

'Oh my master, consider that if a man has prolonged sex with a Prayer-Cushion woman, it involves his total destruction and remaking, for that is the meaning of *fitna*. Having been seduced, the man's soul has to be melted down in order that he may experience the Rapture and it is possible the Rapture may kill him, but whether a man comes out of it alive or not is irrelevant. Long before that, the man has been seduced into total self-abnegation and his original personality has been burnt up in the fires of ecstasy. The thing which walks away from the bed has nothing in common with the man who originally lay down there with a Prayer-Cushion of the Flesh.'

Orkhan had been trying to concentrate on the meaning of what the Vizier was saying, but he found it difficult. The problem was that every time the Vizier said 'woman', or 'women', or 'bed', the tongue in Orkhan's mouth stirred. What did the meaning of an Arabic word matter and what did practices of ancient Balkan sects matter, if only the viper that coiled and uncoiled behind his teeth could be given its drink? It was getting harder and harder to think of anything except soft, white, fleshy thighs.

Finally Orkhan confessed,

'I do not understand. I have no idea what you are talking about.'

'I do not understand it myself,' replied the Vizier. 'Only the women understand these things.'

He was about to say more, but at that moment a girl in a page's uniform came marching up the path and delivered a message to the Vizier. He, having read it, began to argue fiercely with the page girl. Finally he shrugged and dismissed her. Then he turned to Orkhan.

'It seems that Mihrimah awaits her Sultan.'

'Is Mihrimah a person who commands sultans?'

The Vizier did not trouble to reply to this. Instead he said,

'We are going to a different part of the Harem which is distant from the parts you have so far visited. I will tell you a story as we walk.

The story the Vizier told was as follows:

Hundreds of years ago, one of the first of the Sultans, an ancestor of Orkhan's, led his armies against the Kingdom of Nabatea and ravaged it. Nabatea was (and still is) notoriously a foul and idolatorous land, inhabited by sorcerers, poisoners and cannibals, and the Sultan's armies dealt with them accordingly and the Turkish soldiers only withdrew after turning most of the territory into a wasteland. Although the Nabateans were almost all wholly evil, it must be conceded that they did possess the virtue of patience. In the year that their land was devastated by Turkish armies, a girl was born to the King of Nabatea. The king, the proud father, gave orders that poison was to be added to the child's suckling milk. In accordance with his orders, the nipples of the wet-nurse were smeared with the poison. There are different reports of which poison was used – perhaps aconite, perhaps mercury, perhaps arsenic – but, whatever the substance, it was fed to the little girl in the tiniest quantities, so that, instead of the poison killing her, the baby became accustomed to its ingestion, and, as the baby grew into a girl, poison continued to be added to her food, so that every vein of her body was saturated with the deadly stuff.

This was in the great age of the poisoners when

toxicology was the master science. There are no such
poisoners now, alas! But, to return to the girl – Aslan
Khatun was the name of this princess – she had
become a poison damsel and the very saliva from her
lips could burn through porcelain. Once she reached
the marriageable age, the King of Nabatea wrote to
the Ottoman Sultan proposing a perpetual peace
between their two realms and that this peace be con-
firmed by a marriage alliance between his daughter
and the Sultan's heir apparent, Prince Nazim. His
design, of course, was to kill the Sultan's son, for the
moment the prince embraced the princess he would
infallibly die from the poison carried in the juices
of her saliva, or the moisture between her legs.
Her body was so impregnated with poison that
the interior of her vagina was like a nest full of
angry wasps. Sex with a poison damsel is one of the
recognised forms of the Death of the Just Man.

The Ottoman Sultan naively agreed to the king's
proposal and Aslan Khatun set out on the long journey from Nabatea to Istanbul. On the day of her
arrival in that city she was brought before the king
and his son. Aslan Khatun was radiantly beautiful –
literally so, for there was a strange silvery sheen to
her skin. (Perhaps it was arsenic that she had fed
upon, for arsenic is reputed to be good for the skin.)
Prince Nazim fell in love with her at first sight. When
he saw her standing tall and graceful before him, he
knew he needed no other blessing from life, save to be
possessed of her body. And in the course of that
evening's wedding feast, she, very much against her
will, slowly and reluctantly fell in love with him. She

had been trained from birth by the women of the Nabatean court in all the arts of seduction, and though now she did not want to seduce this young man, whom she first thought she liked and then realised she desired madly, nevertheless every word she spoke and every little gesture she made seemed to hint at the delights of love. She knew no other language and so she lured the man she desired and yet did not desire to his doom.

At last, the moment came for Prince Nazim to lead his bride to the nuptial chamber. This was the moment for which Aslan Khatun had been raised, so that she might avenge the wrongs suffered by her native land. But now she realised that she cared nothing about avenging the injuries of Nabatea. Before the amorous prince could lay a hand on her, she warned him to desist. If he valued his life he had to keep away. She went on to explain her father's evil design. 'You may look, but do not touch,' she said, 'for I love you more than I love my father and his poisonous dreams of revenge'.

But Nazim, who was already in love with her, having heard her confession, only became the more besotted with the Nabatean princess. He knew that he loved her, he loved all of her, and if poison was part of her, the fluid that coursed through her blood and her saliva, then that poison was also something to be loved. He swiftly decided that his life was well lost for a moment of loving rapture with this radiant woman. So he said this to Aslan Khatun and, before she could resist, he took her in his arms and embraced her fiercely. Then he kissed her and drank her bitter saliva greedily and in his last remaining moments he went on to ravish her, before expiring in great pain and fierce delight. In the morning the courtiers came and found the prince dead on the nuptial couch. His corpse was already black from the deadly, putrefying liquids which coursed through it. Aslan Khatun sat lamenting beside the bloated body of her lover and, when she asked to be buried alive in the tomb of the man who had been her husband for one night, it was a request which the courtiers were happy to agree to.

As soon as the Vizier had finished this story, Orkan wanted to know why he had told it.

'Does everything have to have reason? It is a fairy-story told for pleasure.'

'Did Barak sleep with a poison damsel?' Orkhan persisted.

'He certainly did not. There is no such thing as a poison damsel. As I said, it is merely a fairy-story. The story of Nazim and and Aslan Khatun is, like the stories of Majnun and Layla, or Khusraw and Shirin, a romance about lovers. Enjoy my story and enjoy your life. You are young, strong and a prince. You still have the capacity for adventure, romance and love. An ageing, hunchbacked dwarf like myself has never had your fortune . . . Yet nature did not make me the way I am. For that I curse my parents. Do you know what a *gloottokoma* is?'

Orkhan indicated that he did not.

'*Gloottokoma* is a Greek word. It means a box which is designed for the making of dwarfs. In my early years as a child in a Greek village I spent almost all the hours of the day in a series of boxes, which were designed to stunt my growth, for my parents had decided that I should be reared as a dwarf and sold for a good price to some king's palace. The less of me there was, the more valuable I would be. Other people in our village were rearing their girls to become concubines. As I remember it, the whole village was composed of slave farms. Similarly, in Egypt we hear that there are specialists in the manufacture of entertaining cripples. In Jezira there are surgeons who are masters of the art of creating 'laughing men' – men whose lips are so distorted that they seem always to be laughing, for in such a manner they may earn a living as cheerful-seeming beggars. There are also craftsmen who specialise in giving boys deformed limbs or giant testicles. Cages and boxes in which monsters like myself are created are scattered throughout the world. This is the rottenness of the age.'

Orkhan thought about this. 'You have not done so badly. You have become Imperial Vizier.

The Vizier smiled,

'Well anyway, you are young, the night is young and you are going to see Mihrimah. Enjoy what is to come for as long as you may.'

They passed down a series of narrow, covered streets, flanked by tiers of cells for the use of concubines and eunuchs. The Vizier stood aside to allow Orkhan to pass through a door and alone descend a flight of steps which led down into a kind of oval pit. There was a rank sort of smell which he was unable to place. A couple of candles had been placed on the floor of the pit, but these flickered in the faint

draught so that it was some time before he was able
to see that the far end of the pit was caged off and
that behind the close-meshed golden grillwork of the
cage stood a veiled and hooded woman.

Orkhan cautiously made his way between the
candles and, pressing against the cage's bars, gazed
at the woman inside. She wore a blouse of white silk
gauze which hung over thin rose-coloured trousers of
damask, embroidered with silver flowers. A broad
scarlet sash ran round her waist and this was fas-
tened with a clasp of diamonds. The woman's feet
were encased in white leather boots studded with
gold. Behind her, at the back of the cage was a door
on which was painted the crudely executed image of
a black cat.

Orkhan spoke first,

'Lady, who are you? And who has imprisoned you
in a cage? Shall I set you free?'

' My name is Mihrimah which means "Sun-Moon",
but my title is that of Durrah, the "Parrot". Nobody
has imprisoned me. Rather I have arranged to have
myself locked in here for your own protection, lest I
kill you.' The woman's voice was sweet, but, seeing
how Orkhan pressed against the golden bars, she
became insistent, 'If you value your life, do not
attempt to break into the cage. Instead, sit down and
I will explain to you why the "Parrot" is in the cage,
as well as the meaning of my name. Sit down, listen
and admire.'

Orkhan obeyed and Mihrimah continued,

'We who are Prayer-Cushions of the Flesh teach
and test incessantly, but we never repeat ourselves

and no man in our care ever experiences the same orgasm twice. Anadil having given you your first lesson, it falls to me to take you over that same ground again. Since I am your second designated concubine, I take the title of Durrah, the "Parrot", and I repeat what you have experienced before and I go over it, in order to make sure that you have understood it. And yet we never repeat ourselves, so that, whereas Anadil only spoke of externals, I point to their inner meanings. Just as Anadil's beauty is only a shadow of mine, so in her prattling she served you merely the outer husks of sense, while I deliver the inner kernel, for foolish Anadil knows the names of things, but she does not know their meaning . . . .'

Orkhan thought of Anadil and her jangling jewellery and daft lessons on the parts of the body. Mihrimah, pale in the shadows, continued to talk on and on about how he had so far learnt only about sex and not about love. Yet sex was a necessary preliminary, a dim adumbration of the Rapture that lay ahead. Sex with stupid people, such as Anadil and her washerwoman, was good spiritual discipline for a man. She was saying that on the following day he should go and seek the pardon of those ladies, for that was the lover's way of abjection . . .

Orkhan sat listening quite contentedly as Mihrimah walked about her cage, talking about the mysteries of desire and extinction. Man was born to love the transient and the passing, the flesh that grew raddled and hung slackly. It was only because fleshly beauty was passing that it was truly loveable. Of course, nothing Mihrimah was saying about mystical sex made any sense at all to him, but she had a lovely voice and her vanity was charming – as was the waggle of her hips as she paced about her cage. He was happy to sit and watch this creature forever. All the same, it occurred to him that Mihrimah would have all her occult nonsense about lunar rapture, the exaltation of servitude and whatnot rapidly knocked out of her, if only he could get his cock inside her. He had just decided that Mihrimah was a nice, ordinary young woman and that her mad notions were the natural outcome of not having been with a man – of having spent too long in a Harem which was not being serviced by a proper man – when she began to speak of the Dolorous Gaze,

'Before the end, you will long for death, if only to free you from the Rapture. For the moment, you behold me dressed, hooded and veiled, lest the splendour of my naked beauty blind you. I have covered myself as an act of mercy to you, lest you die of the Rapture. But now, if you are ready, I will intensify your desire by allowing you to gaze successively on the most dangerously desirable parts of my body.'

Orkhan having nodded, Mihrimah began to fumble with the lacing of her blouse. She knelt to expose her breasts and, supporting them with her hands, she thrust them forwards for Orkhan's attention. As she did so there was a strange trumpeting sound in the distance.

'These are the first subjects of contemplation,' she said. 'What did Anadil call them?'

'She called them her moons,' replied Orkhan.

63

'She was right to do so, yet what is the meaning of that?'

Mihrimah knelt as close as she could to him, so that the tips of her breasts brushed against the golden bars of the cage. Even the eyeholes of her veil of black velvet were covered with a fine trellis of threads. Orkhan toyed with the idea that her face might be ravaged by leprosy or otherwise hideously disfigured.

Mihrimah's melodious voice continued to discourse learnedly about her breasts being the figures of moons in a sexual cosmos and, like all things connected with the moon, subject to change and decay. They had to be loved not only for what they were, but for what they would become – withered dugs. But the breasts were also doves' eggs and they were pomegranates too. Above all, they were to be reverenced as the Lesser Prayer-Cushions, on which man might find his solace and spiritual salvation – the parts here standing for the whole of a woman's body which is the Greater Prayer-Cushion. All men, in longing to return to the breast, are actually longing to return to the Divinity. The twin moons were divinely-fashioned navigational aids on this journey of mystical return.

While Mihrimah spoke of domes of alabaster lit by rays of lunar mystery, Orkhan gazed on her breasts as if hypnotised. They were indeed very pretty, but he thought that they more closely resembled blind puppies who were in need of petting than they did mystic moons. He felt something stirring at the base of his spine.

'Look at my breasts! Really look at them!' Mihrimah insisted. 'They seem to offer themselves to you, whether I wish it or not. They are soft and vulnerable and yet they seem to threaten you, do they not? How can this be?'

Seeing that Orkhan made no reply, she pointed at him and continued,

'Or if you cannot truly see my breasts as they should be seen, then gaze upon yourself – so hard, so tight, so compact, but with that cock you cannot control. You are very strong, a hard man, but yet you are trapped by my weakness. Seduction is nothing but the trick of the weak to capture the strong. The strong always yearns to discharge its strength in softness and become weak. But you must become weaker yet. It is time for the second stage in the discipline of the gaze.'

And, so saying, Mihrimah threw back her hood and stripped off the veil, to reveal a mass of golden hair framing a calm and pleasantly rounded face, which, in the dim candlelight glowed like the pale moon. She smiled at Orkhan as she lectured on herself and especially her face. Her hair's tresses were a net to trap the lover. He, the lover, was a nightingale trapped in a rose-garden in flames. The nightingale and the rose-garden were both alike doomed to perish and they would achieve union only in the mingling of their ashes. Was it nobler to love beauty or to be beautiful? Which had the finer part – the nightingale or the rose-garden?

Though she went on speaking of the high mysteries of her sex, Orkhan as he contemplated her face, breasts and shoulders, was fantasising about what it would be like to have the woman's flesh actually under his hands. Desire was building within him. The pain between his legs was so intense that he did not think he would be able to rise again, unless he speedily achieved some relief. He was only startled out of his brooding frustration when she announced,

'Now I shall show you my other face.' She turned away and, unclasping the sash, she lowered her trousers, talking all the while.

'In this way,' she said 'I conquer by humbling myself before you, for the way of the lover is self-abnegation without hope of the gratification of desire. This is the penultimate stage in the discipline of the gaze before you shall behold me fully naked. Then look on my bottom and marvel!'

Orkhan did as he was told. She swayed and shifted her weight from one foot to the other, so that the heavy cheeks of her bottom rose and fell, gleaming in the brilliant light. Her bottom was, he learned, like the breasts in that it was a figure of the moon and governed by the moon. It was pale and luminous and, like the moon, it could destroy man's reason.

Orkhan decided that he preferred Mihrimah's bottom to her breasts, for her bottom had an imperious quality that her more tentative breasts lacked. So, as she sought to instruct him about the sand dunes over which a lover's hands must travel, about the soft, white clouds which veiled the Divinity from man, and about the astral thrall exerted by the bottom and the bitter mystery of its dark abyss, Orkhan furtively raised his robe and in a quiet fever set to masturbating. He was desperate to come to a climax and, if possible, to do so before Mihrimah should turn to him again, but just as he was ejaculating in hot thick spurts, she turned to him and cried out in dismay. An instant later the door behind her swung open and a strong gust of wind swept through the pit and Orkhan was plunged into darkness. It was as if a vast black-gloved hand had descended, extinguishing the candles.

Another woman's voice, not Mihrimah's cried out, fierce and terrible,

'Unhappy the man who has failed the test of the Dolorous Gaze! Leave him to darkness and shame, the prisoner of his lust.'

CHAPTER FIVE

IN THE GIRAFFE HOUSE

The sounds of lamentation increased briefly, then died away. Orkhan did not move, but sat in pitch darkness. Where, after all, should he go? Passionate, brightly-coloured images chased one another about in his head – he had witnessed so many unfamiliar sights, so many curious tableaux, all in the matter of a few hours. Some of the things he had seen he did not even have a name for. Other things were as yet only names. The Rapture was still only a name. At least he had saved himself from that. Eventually his eyelids fluttered and drooped and he slumped back onto the stone floor and slept where he had been sitting. Even while he slept, the viper in his mouth flicked restlessly from side to side.

He was woken by the sounds of rustling, scratching and muttering. He opened his eyes and beheld the daylight streaming in from a lantern in the roof of the pit. He looked into the cage expecting to see Mihrimah, but there, where Mihrimah had stood on the previous evening, was an old woman in a coarse, brown robe. The woman's head was sunk so low that it hardly rose above her shoulders. On reflection, it was more like a skull than a head, for the thin hair did not cover it, skin stretched over angular bones and the eyes were set deep within the bones. A thin wispy beard sprouted from the woman's jaw, the jut

71

of which was accentuated by her toothlessness. Orkhan toyed with the notion that he was indeed gazing at Mihrimah, that he had just been asleep for seventy years and that it was to this that the discipline of the Dolorous Gaze had brought him. The woman looked down on him briefly before resuming her work, scattering straw over the floor of the cage.

Then, when she had finished this task, she shuffled out through the door at the back of the cage. There were muffled shouts. Then the door opened again and a panther padded in. The panther was followed by a muscular girl with close-cropped red hair. She was dressed in black leather – skirt, laced bodice and gloves. Her feet were bare and she carried a whip. She did not notice Orkhan, for all her attention was on the panther, which she baited with her whip, lightly flicking at the creature's nose and muzzle. The panther, like a kitten confronted with a ball of string, snarled, lashed its tail and sought to catch at the thong with its talons. At last the girl tired of this game and cast the whip away. The panther leapt towards her and together they rolled over the straw. Orkhan cried out, but he was ignored, as the girl and the panther tumbled over one another. She was momentarily astride the supple, rippling, velvety back of the beast, before he slipped out from under her and in a moment she was lying under him. Her skirt had ridden up and she was wearing nothing underneath. The creature stood over her, dripping saliva on to her body, seeming to devour her with his stony green eyes, before inclining his head to lash her face with his rough tongue. She reached up to clasp his neck and together they rolled over once more. The panther began to purr as she stroked his stomach.

Suddenly she cried out. She had just noticed that her game with the beast was being observed by Orkhan. She leapt up, as if embarrassed to be discovered at play. She strode over to the bars of the cage, with the panther slinking close beside her. Orkhan, who remained sitting, caught a blast of the creature's breath, which was both sweet and foul.

'Who are you?' said the girl, looking down on Orkhan.

'My name is Orkhan. I am your Sultan'.

The girl seemed neither surprised nor impressed.

'I am Roxelana,' she said, as she fumbled in her bodice, before producing a key at the end of a chain. 'Roxelana means "the Russian".' And she gave the panther a final stroke before picking up her whip, unlocking the cage door and joining Orkhan on the other side. The trapped and abandoned panther gazed balefully up at Orkhan.

'I call him Babur,' said Roxelana. She stood close beside Orkhan and gazed down on her former playmate. Her face was smudged and there was a scratch of blood on her shoulders. She smelled of sweat and the panther. Her voice was husky as she had not yet recovered from her exertions and her breasts rose and fell as she struggled to regain her breath. Those breasts seemed to Orkhan to more closely resemble extra muscles than any conventional feature of a woman's body. Roxelana was, like her panther, a mass of sinew and muscle.

'Are you one of the concubines of the Harem?' he asked doubtfully.

She let out a laugh that was half delighted, half scornful,

'Ha! I could not bear to have anything to do with the Harem women. No, I am one of the animal girls who work in the Imperial Zoo. I would much rather serve animals than the ninnies of the Harem.'

'There is an Imperial Zoo? Where is it?'

She gave him a curious look,

'It is here. You are in it. Why else should you be talking to an animal girl and standing in front of a cage containing a panther? This is Babur's cage.' And she pointed to a brass plaque attached to the bars at the top of the cage. The inscription in swirls of decorative calligraphy announced that THIS IS THE PANTHER, MARVELLOUS IN HIS BEAUTY, WHOSE BREATH IS SWEET AS THE SPICES OF JAVA.

'But last night there was no panther,' said Orkhan who was wondering if he was going mad. 'Last night I saw a woman who said she was called Mihrimah stand behind those bars and start to undress herself in front of me.'

'Ah! So it was Mihrimah? That girl thinks that the sun shines out of her arse, that moonlight issues from her cunt and she believes that she is the mother of cosmic mysteries, that her body is an orchard, a sea, a desert, a fountain, a mirror, a mystic robe and, at the end of it all, a bloody Prayer-Cushion for man to kneel on as he prays before the Holy of Holies. She's mad, quite mad . . . She also thinks that she can walk into the Zoo and do what she likes, take over its cages, turn out the animals, give orders to the staff. The insolence of those courtesans and dancing girls takes my breath away. The reality is that Mihrimah and the rest of the concubines are good for nothing, except fucking – and doing embroidery. But they lie about in the Harem and thoughts of sex rot away their soft insides and eat up their little brains. All that Prayer-Cushion rubbish that they preach . . . it's only the product of not enough proper sex. Cooped up in their cramped dormitories, they pleasure one another and fantasise about men, but all they ever see is eunuchs.' She paused to calm herself and get her breath back, before continuing, 'But we are all prisoners here, women, eunuchs and animals. Of course, the main zoo is over at the Hippodrome. This is only a little zoo within the Harem for the pleasure of the Sultan's concubines. We have wild boars, gazelles, porcupines, a buffalo, a small herd of giraffes . . . Two of the giraffes are homosexual and they use their necks to court one another.'

She placed her gloved hand in his. Her eyes sparkled.

'Come and see the homosexual giraffes.'

She led him up out of the pit and down a roofed and cobbled street that twisted between cages and storerooms. They came to a low doorway over which was written, THESE ARE THE SULTAN'S HUNTERS WHO SIT ON THE GLOVES OF LADIES AND WAIT TO BRING DEATH FROM THE SKIES. Roxelana ducked in and Orkhan followed her through the imperial mews. Hawks in plumed leather helmets stirred restlessly on their perches. Roxelana explained that this was a short cut. Then they emerged out through another low door into the high-roofed and airy giraffe stable. HERE ARE THE HAPPY OFFSPRING OF THE MATING OF CAMELS AND LEOPARDS WHO ARE CALLED GIRAFFES

'Everywhere in the Harem is so cramped,' said Roxelana. 'Apart from the hammam, I think this is the biggest building there is.'

A giraffe lazily sought to entwine his neck round that of his neighbour. Hands on hips, Roxelana stood gazing up at the animals in rapt delight. Orkhan followed her gaze. The creatures did not resemble the giraffes in the bestiary which he used to study in the Cage. They were strange, but then everything was so strange to him, and surely Roxelana was the strangest creature in her zoo. She slapped the flank of one of the languid giraffes, seeking to urge it on in its seduction, then turned to Orkhan and smiled. He was certain that he had never seen such strong white teeth or such brilliant eyes before. Suddenly he realised that he was desperate for her – desperate to feed off her energy and drink from her overflowing life.

'Aren't they wonderful?' she said, pointing at the animals who had begun to nuzzle one another.

'Never mind the giraffes,' he said. 'What about me?'

He yanked at her arm and pulled her down on to a heap of straw. She pulled up her skirt, ready for him.

'Now, quickly. If you want me, it must be now, before the jinns come.'

Those were the last words that it was possible to

make sense of, as she started to moan noisily. She gestured to him to make haste as he struggled out of his robe. Even in the dung-scented air of the giraffe stable, he could smell Roxelana. Her skin, caked as it was with dried sweat and saliva, stank. Also, it seemed that she had used rancid butter to give her helmet of red hair more of a sheen. The insides of her thighs were moist and smelt of cat. Like Anadil, she was clean-shaven between the legs. Driven by the cravings of the viper, he tried to thrust his head down there, but she was impatient.

'Not like that. I want something bigger than your tongue inside me.' She wrestled under him and pulled him up and grabbed at his cock. She reminded Orkhan of his brother princes with whom he used to wrestle. Powerfully aroused, he entered her masterfully. However, the sensation of mastery hardly lasted more than a moment, for she so fiercely bucked and thrashed under him. Her eyes rolled and her teeth were gritted. Finally, she made such a great heave that he was unable to stay inside her. He withdrew and lay beside her and waited for her frenzy to abate.

'I am accursed!' she wailed. 'Forgive me, master, yet it is not my fault.' Now she was weeping. 'It is the fault of the jinns. Whenever I even think about sex, the jinns enter my body and possess it. It is the jinns who make me do such frightful things.'

She buried her head in the straw and continued to weep. Then, as her sobbing subsided, she raised her tear-stained face to Orkhan and said,

'I need to be purified. You can purify me. You can whip the jinns out of me. Please, I need to have the jinns driven out of me. They cannot bear the pain, but I, Roxelana, can bear anything. If you flog me, O Sultan, I promise you that you will then be able to enjoy my body as is your right.'

Now she was in a new fever of impatience. She stepped out of her black skirt and with trembling hands set to unlacing her bodice. The bodice fell to the ground and, as she turned away from him, Orkhan saw that her broad shoulders were already covered with a light tracery of scars. Then she turned to him again and presented him with the whip.

'Flog me now,' she implored. 'I am begging you for it. I need it.' And she turned away and bent to present her back for chastisement.

Orkhan struck at her a couple of times, but she was not satisfied.

'Harder. It must be harder. You have to draw my blood, for the jinns are in my blood. You have to let them out.'

Her broad bottom seemed made for whipping and he struck at it again and again. Ugly red weals began to break up its milky smoothness. For the first time since his release from the Cage, Orkhan felt himself to be truly a sultan and, as he continued to lash out at Roxelana, he began to fantasise about how he would deal with Anadil and the other ladies of the Harem. He worked a little way up her back before pausing for breath.

Then she said,

'You must be able to do better than this. Harem girls have whipped me harder than you have. Come on, I really want to feel it – your touch of mastery.'

Her words had the effect she desired. Orkhan struck out at her in a frenzy. Now she was crying and calling out to him, but his rage was such that it was some time before he could hear that she was begging him to desist. He stopped and she turned to kneel in front of him and kiss the whip.

'Thank you, master. Now you may do with me what you wish,' and she lay back once more on the straw. This time it was different. The devils having departed, she docilely lay back and allowed herself to be penetrated. She embraced him tenderly as he moved inside her.

She sighed as he came within her,

'Thank you master,' she said again and kissed him hungrily. 'It has always been hard for me, for the jinns that come into my body will not allow me to acknowledge the supremacy of a man. Now at last I am at peace.'

And Orkhan observed that her eyes were dulled, sated. Yet, it now occurred to him that, with her back such a bloody mess, she must have been moving on a bed of agony as she gave herself to him.

'Did I hurt you?' he asked foolishly.

'Of course you did – a little, but women are used to pain. They are better capable of bearing it than men,' and she smiled patronisingly at him.

'I do not believe that. Everyone knows that men are stronger, tougher and better able to bear pain.'

'With respect, O master, perhaps men think they know that, but I do not. Women are born equipped to face far more pain than men, for nature has prepared them in advance to suffer the travails of childbirth. And every month I experience such pain that you cannot imagine. Your whipping was a little nothing by comparison.' The brightness was back in her eyes again and she looked at him mischievously. 'You could never stand such a whipping as the one I received from your hands.'

'You are being absurd, Roxelana. I should certainly be much better able to endure it than you were.'

'Then let us try it, shall we?'

Orkhan hesitated. Why, after all, should he submit to being whipped by one of his animal girls?

Seeing him hesitate, she urged him on,

'Come on my lord! It is only a game, like my game with the panther. Such sports make us feel more alive, for, though we may walk through life as if we walked in a dream, the flick of the whip can wake us up. Turn and turn about,' she insisted. 'You will enjoy it. Trust me.' And she gave him a brilliant smile.

Tempted by the challenge, seduced by her smile, he agreed. Then she led him to a corner of the stables, and pointed to a pair of manacles which were attached by chains to the wall.

'Put these on,' she said.

Once again, he balked. Now she was angry and stamped her foot.

'You have to wear these. Otherwise it is not fair. It will not be a real challenge, if you can cry off at any moment, or turn round and snatch the whip from me and start beating me again. You have to trust me. You have to trust me, as I trusted you. Believe me, you will find that half your delight comes from trusting the lady with the whip. Trust me, it will only be a

80

gentle whipping – like a series of butterfly kisses on your body.'

Orkhan offered his wrists to the manacles.

'We sometimes put an unruly monkey in these,' she explained, as she snapped them shut.

'Now its my turn!' she cried and the whip sang in the air.

Orkhan was unable to stop his body wincing as the thong made its first incision in his flesh. She was more skilled with the whip than he had been and the blows fell fast and accurately.

He heard her cry out,

'Oh my beloved, I swear to you that I am only marking your body because I desire it. My whip is making a map to guide my loving kisses.'

Then suddenly the blows increased yet further in ferocity and she seemed to be talking to herself in a foreign language, in which guttural words mingled with groans and hisses. It was not long before Orkhan, half swooning, slumped against the floor. Then she was upon him, pressing herself against his back and licking his blood.

'You are mad,' he groaned.

'So I am,' she replied. 'My jinns have come back and they want your blood. Oh my beloved master, forgive me, but I cannot hold back from this.' And she resumed kissing and licking at his wounds.

At last she raised her face from his body and gave a deep sigh. When she next spoke, her voice was calm and gentle,

'Now the kiss of the whip has taught you a little about the strange delight of suffering. Even so, you still have no idea about the pain of being a woman. In order to really make love to a woman, you will have to learn what it feels like to be one and to be made love to as a woman.' She ran a hand over his hair.

'Don't go away, will you?'

And she was gone, leaving Orkhan chained on the floor of the giraffe stable.

When she returned, she nudged him with her foot and used it to turn him as far over as his chains would allow. Looking up at Roxelana, he first noticed that her mouth was rimmed with blood. Then he saw a large, greased and gleaming red thing attached by an intricate array of straps to the lower part of her belly and he moaned in dread.

'This dildo,' she said, pointing to the thing 'consists of a unicorn's horn sheathed in red Cordovan leather. It is only used for the deflowering of virgins.'

Then she briefly caressed his mouth with her foot, before kicking and turning him again, so that he was lying face down on the straw. She prodded him again with her foot.

'I want you kneeling.'

'When I am free you will pay for this.'

But, she struck at him with the butt of the whip and he did as he was told.

'How will I pay for it?' Roxelana demanded sarcastically. 'Have me flogged, will you?'

As she spoke, she knelt over his bottom and spat on her hands before using the spittle to moisten the passage of her instrument in advance. Then she mounted him and rammed the dildo in, or rather, she attempted to, but Orkhan was very tight.

So she began to whisper hotly in his ear, begging him to relax and calling him her 'handsome darling' and her 'plaything'. But all the while she continued to thrust with the horn between her legs. It felt like a great fist which, in beating its way upwards, was seeking to cleave Orkhan from bottom to top. It was as if he was being impaled on the shaft of the animal girl. It was as if he was carrying the woman inside him. It was as if he was being possessed by a dark demon who would not be denied entrance.

There was a final shudder as she at last succeeded in driving the horn into him. Pleasure and pain, exquisitely compounded, surged within him, overwhelming his will, so that he suffered orgasm.

Roxelana stroked his head. He could feel her breasts pressing against his back. He was in agony, and yet he longed for nothing more than to be able to turn to embrace his violator.

'Now, my Sultan, a door has been opened for the Holy Rapture,' she whispered, and giving the dildo a final twist, she continued 'It is possible that you are now ready to yield to the total extinction which is perfect love.'

She might have said more, but at that moment they heard the sound of women's voices outside the stables. Roxelana thereupon swiftly unstrapped herself from the dildo's harness and slipped away. Orkhan briefly fainted.

When he came to, he saw that Perizade was kneeling beside him and drawing gently on the harness of the dildo to extract it.

'Yeeugh, it's all bloody!' she exclaimed 'One of the

animal girls has been sporting with you. Anadil is waiting outside, but she must not see you like this. Most of the concubines and their servants have been hunting for you. At first we feared that you might have tried to flee the Harem, but then we thought that you would not and could not leave the Harem, because you are already addicted to what is between our legs. Finally we realised that you must still be in the zoo and that one of the animal girls must have spirited you away for her pleasure.'

She rolled Orkhan over carefully. He tried to speak, but could not. He tried to stand, but slumped forward with his head on Perizade's heavy breasts. She laid him back on the straw. Her heavy breasts swung low over his face.

'You see, you cannot escape me. I am your destiny.'

'Perizade, please help me,' he gasped in his chains.

'I think that I know what will revive you. Your viper must be thirsty, isn't it?' she asked solicitously, and, without waiting for an answer, she drew up her skirt and straddled him, lowering her plump fleshy thighs on to his face. Once more the thirsty viper slithered its way in to slake its thirst in the Tavern of the Perfume-Makers.

Then she rose from his face and cast about to find the key for the manacles and his robe. When Orkhan was dressed and on his feet, she took his hand.

'We will not say exactly what happened – even to Anadil. It would never do for the imperial concubines to hear of this. But you need to be cleaned up. It is time for the hammam.'

CHAPTER SIX

FAIRY INTRIGUES

A great philosopher once observed that the conversation of a pretty concubine is like the study of history. Both are endlessly delightful, but one learns nothing from either. Anadil was waiting outside. She carried a parasol and was wearing a silk pink robe and gloves.

She started talking the moment Orkhan came within earshot.

'There you are at last. Have you been sporting with one of the animal girls? All the princes have been the same. They were like animals too and when they come out of the Cage all they could think about was rubbing flesh against flesh. I say that it is the job of we Harem girls to school you men in the arts of a more courtly love.

And she offered him her gloved hand to be kissed.

'And keep your head down. I do not like to be looked at all the time. As we walk along, you must tell me how pretty I am and you may propose small ways in which you can be of service to me.'

As Orkhan walked close beside her, he felt himself drowning in Anadil's perfume. She told him that it was ylang-ylang. He thought that it was redolent of the tomb – of memorial stones, thick carpets, funereal chants and burning censers – bitter and ominous. Perizade, who was a little ahead of them, said that the shortest way to the hammam, would be through the mews, but Anadil rejected this advice, saying that Perizade's route would only take them further into the zoo. So she gave the directions, in between instructing Orkhan on the discipline of the gaze and about how he might advance from the profane sphere of sex to the sacred sphere of love. Orkhan listened with half an ear. He was admiring the flare of Perizade's hips and the undulation of her walk.

With her free hand Anadil tapped him on the arm, 'I hope that you enjoyed your sex with the animal girl. From now on, until the moment of your death, there will be no more sex of any kind . . . That girl now was she as pretty as me?'

'She was not.'

'That is not a proper answer. You must list the ways in which she was not as pretty as me.'

Orkhan dutifully compiled a list of compliments to please Anadil, but his eyes were on Perizade and his mind was elsewhere again. Something Roxelana had said made him apprehensive, yet he could not remember what it was. But by now, everything made him apprehensive – Anadil's perfume, her reference to the moment of his death, the desolation of the Harem. In the distance, they could hear the eerie singing of the eunuchs. But the route they took, through narrow corridors running between abandoned reception chambers and lumber rooms, was entirely deserted. Orkhan was thinking, as he walked with Anadil and Perizade, that the way the women had been showing off their bodies to him and the relentless sequence of fuckings and floggings . . . it seemed to him as if the Harem had been conjured up out of the fantasies of the Princes in the Cage. It was as if the Harem was built of nothing more substantial than sexual dreams of the men who were its prisoners.

They came to the Alleyway of the Dwarfs, a double row of kennel-like dwellings for the court dwarfs. Anadil stuck her head in a few of the kennels to see if any of the dwarf families were at home, but their rooms too were deserted and there was no one around to give them directions. Although Perizade had been in this place before, she could not remember how to get from there to the hammam. By now it was perfectly apparent that they were hopelessly lost and Orkhan could not disguise his impatience.

'If I were you, I would not be in such a hurry to reach your destination,' said Perizade sadly.

'Perizade is right,' said Anadil. 'Enjoy the air and the changing scenery. It is a nice walk we are having'.

But they had only taken a few more steps along the Alleyway when they found their passage blocked by a giant figure, black in a black robe and turban, who carried a scimitar and towered over the dwarf-kennels. He favoured them with an enormous smile,

'Anadil, darling!'

'We are saved!' she exclaimed. 'It's Emerald.'

'Have you any chocolates for me?' asked Emerald.

'Not today, Emerald. Let us not talk about that now. This is your new master, the Sultan Orkhan, and this is my washerwoman, Perizade. We are all on the way to the hammam, Emerald. You can show us the way.'

He bowed his head,

'To hear is to obey. But first, perhaps, you will honour me by joining me in my rooms for coffee.'

The suite of the *Kislar Agha*, or Chief Black Eunuch, was attractively furnished. They sat on low padded benches and drank coffee. The shelves above their heads were crowded with goldfish bowls. A bluish-grey cat appeared and leapt onto Emerald's lap.

'Azrael, named after his grandfather, the Angel of Death.'

Emerald got a hookah alight and puffed at it, in between sips of coffee and conversation. But after a while, he put the mouthpiece of the hookah down and turned to look thoughtfully at Orkhan,

'I was not born a eunuch,' he said.

Orkhan indicated that he had surmised as much.

'I grew up a prince in the heart of Africa. Any of the women in our tribe were mine for the asking. Only my brother, who was king of the tribe took precedence over me. In particular, there was a beautiful woman called Rasya. I recall that she had haunches to match the finest specimens of our cattle. I used to lie awake sleepless, envying him his nights with Rasya. But one day the elders of the tribe presented themselves before my brother and accused him of being so besotted with this woman that he was neglecting affairs of state. A lesser man might have been angry at being so admonished by his councillors, but my brother was a great king. So he had slaves summon Rasya. Then she came hurrying to him, swaying and all glorious in her finery and she stood before my brother looking at him with loving eyes. He asked the elders to admire her and, one by one, they each admitted that they too would be neglecting affairs of state, if they had been blest with such a beautiful bedmate. Then my brother, the king, nodded and asked Rasya to come closer. She did as she was told and he swiftly cut her throat with his dagger, soaking himself in her blood as he did so. "I am master of myself, just as I am master of my tribe," he said and with that he dismissed the elders.'

'Naturally, this scene made a great impression on me. But soon there was another very beautiful woman installed in Rasya's place. Makala, I think she was called. She lasted only a few months. This time the councillors did not even have to complain, before my brother, fearing that he was becoming too dependent on her, killed her. But then there was another woman . . . and another. I went away and thought. I was very like my brother and I too feared that I might become obsessed with a woman – or women. And the problem was one not just for me and my brother. All the men in our tribe went about maddened by sex. Moreover, there were not enough desirable women to go around. Things had got to the point that the men of our tribe would go to the river in the hope of sex with crocodiles. (It seems foolish now, but we were all young then.) You know that the female crocodile when she is preparing to mate turns over on her back so that the male may mount her. Whenever they saw that happening, the men of my tribe would rush out and kill or at least drive off the male. The female finds it very difficult to get back to her normal position, so then we would take it in turns to mount her, while she thrashed helplessly about. I had sex with crocodiles twice. I recall how foolish they looked as I caressed their throats. It was supposed to be lucky to do so – an augury of success in one's future career and so it has proved for me, for now I am Chief Eunuch of the Ottoman Harem.'

Emerald sucked in his breath and looked proudly round him, before continuing,

'But I digress. I was about to describe the manner of my becoming a eunuch. I realised that if I was not to remain the emotional prey of any passing woman – or crocodile – a more root-and-branch solution would be necessary. I did not want to pass through life without reflecting. Rather, I wanted to direct my future according to the principles of pure reason. I wanted to use the head that was between my shoulders to guide me in my destiny and I did not want a second head, which was between my legs, telling me to do mad things and countermanding the first head. I needed to escape the prison that my sex had made for me and to be free of the rise and fall of my cock.'

'So I paid to be made a eunuch. It was not cheap and it was not without pain. I had a complete job done. Both the cock and the testicles were removed, so I am one of the *sandali*, or clean-cut eunuchs. I was buried up to my head in sand for three days to cauterise the wound and I had nothing to drink all that time. But it was worth it. I was not against women, you understand. I liked women. I still do. It was sex I was against – all that ridiculous jigggling up and down and those messy fluids. Even so, things have not quite worked out as I had planned . . . '

'Emerald!' said Anadil warningly.

'Ah no, I was thinking about the time of the peris. That was before your time, Anadil. This was in the days when Bayezit still ruled and before our present Valide Sultan had reached even the rank of Parrot. This was when I entered the Harem, for, once I had had myself castrated, I decided to take advantage of my new state and, thinking to advance myself in life, I thought that I should seek to become one of the Imperial slaves. Things went well for me and it was not long before I was purchased in Cairo by one of Sultan Bayezit's agents and brought to Istanbul, where I was inducted into the service of the Harem. I was still young, but despite my youth, as a *sandali* – a clean-cut man – I had a certain status and I commanded respect amongst those eunuchs who had only had their balls cut off. As soon as I arrived, I was put in charge of security, my job being to prevent men from having access to the ladies of the Harem – all men other than the Sultan, of course. However, I soon found that this job of mine was really a sinecure, for anyone foolish enough to make the attempt to smuggle their way into the Harem was easily intercepted long before I could even get a sniff of them. The Janissary guards in the Outer Courtyard of the Palace mounted regular and vigilant patrols to protect the virtue of the ladies within the Harem.'

'It was true that during the reign of Bayezit's father, a couple of young men had succeeded in penetrating the Harem several times in the disguise of dressmakers. But eventually their imposture was discovered and the whole matter secretly and summarily dealt with. How exactly it was dealt with was not known until some five or six months later, when a diver, one of those who swim in the Bosphorus and make a living from scavenging in the sunken wrecks, was diving off Palace Point. The water there is quite shallow but murky, so it was hard to see in. However, the salvage divers have a trick for this. When they plunge in, they do so with a mouthful of olive oil. Then, when they have made their way to the bottom, they let out the oil and look through it. The oil is like a lamp in the dark waters. So the diver let out his oil some way below the surface off Palace Point and then, looking through the great golden gob of oil which shook in the currents of the Bosphorus, he saw weighted sacks resting on the sandy bottom and they too undulated in the currents and it was plain to the diver that the forms which filled the sacks were, or at least had been, human. He returned to the surface and advised his fellow swimmers against thinking of salvaging in that particular stretch of water.'

'Those were great and fierce days. But all that was in the past. In my own time, no one has got past the Janissaries – no human being that is. So after a while I began to get complacent and even a little lazy in my job as guardian of the virtue of the Harem. I was young and the girls were young and pleasant. After a few months, however, I started noticing white stains on some of the sheets in the dormitories. I taxed the concubines whose sheets were so suspiciously marked. They were all glib and smirking. Why, they replied, those were nothing but the stains left by egg whites! It was their new passion late at night – to eat raw eggs in bed. Well, I was a young and inexperienced eunuch, but even so I was doubtful. Why, after all, did the yolks of the eggs leave no stains? At about the same time, I was slowly becoming aware of hearing a tinkling sound only just within the limits of the audible. Then my skin would prickle. This did not happen all the time, but it was happening more and more often.'

'I continued to make surprise inspections of the dormitories, but never did I find a concubine in the arms of a young man – nor for that matter did I ever catch them eating raw eggs. I might have let things drop, were it not for the fact that I was noticing that some of the young girls were looking haggard and pale. I would walk in on them unannounced and I would find them, singly or together, softly moaning and writhing about on the floor or on a mattress for no visible reason. As you know, Bayezit used to favour strapping, vital young women and we were at pains only to buy the healthiest specimens in the slave market. But now his Harem seemed drained of all vitality. The girls were not even interested in the dear old Carpet of Mirth any more and those who greeted me on my rounds of inspection were often wild-eyed and sweaty. The Sultan also was in no better state. I noticed that his hands had become clammy and they shook slightly, like leaves in a breeze.'

'Then one day a couple of the youngest concubines

came to me and complained that they were having difficulty in seeing. They were afraid that they were going blind. I realised then in a flash how stupid I must be not to have seen immediately what the trouble was. No wonder the concubines were having problems with their vision!'

Emerald paused for solemn effect,

'The whole Harem was infested with peris.'

Anadil snorted, but Emerald continued,

'I believe that I am the only person in this room ever to have seen a peri. They are by no means easy things to see. They are like the jinns, but they are smaller. A jinn may often be bigger than a man and sometimes he or she will find it a tight fit to squeeze into a man's body. But the peri is a different matter. Oh who can see the peris? The largest is no bigger than the top of my thumb here. Their appearance is as faint as dreams, but madder than dreams. And they are so fast, like mercury racing over the surface of things, looking for resting places, but never finding them, all the time in and out of pitchers, hiding in eyebrows, exploring the lingerie chests, dancing on pillows, swinging on cobwebs, curdling milk, scavenging in ants' nests, dancing from one hiding place to the next, teasing the eyes of those who try to look on them. I could have a troop of peris dancing on the back of my hand and not be aware of them until I thought about it – the drumming of their feet being no more than itching on my skin.'

'I know that there is the blood of peris in my family,' said Perizade. 'That is why I am able to tell the future.'

Anadil smiled, but Emerald was stern,

'Fairy blood is not a thing to boast about.'

And he continued,

'It was no wonder that some of the concubines were starting to go blind. The peris were so small and, besides, one needed to squint to see them and they were as nimble as thought. I have observed that sometimes for sport they would plunge into a perfumed bead of sweat on a concubine's flesh and in such a manner they would travel fast as a quicksilver pearl down her body. A marvellous things to see – and all but impossible to catch at. A man could be as fast as a fishing cormorant and still find himself snatching at air.'

'Now you,' said Emerald, pointing at Orkhan, 'I know that you really are a big man, almost as tall as the door of the room you entered by. But your image is a different matter. Your image has to shrink to enter my eyeball, so that I can see you. That is right, is it not? So it is that I see you as a little mannikin, no bigger than my eyeball. Nevertheless, not being mad, I know that you really are a big man. The peris, now . . . the peris are different. Their image neither shrinks nor grows. A peri's image is always the same size as its actual body, which is smaller than an eyeball and so hard to see. I could always tell when a concubine was watching a peri, as her pupils would dilate so as to accommodate the tiny creature's image.'

As Emerald paused to puff at the hookah, it suddenly struck Orkhan that the blacks of the eunuch's own pupils were preternaturally large. Emerald blew a few smoke-rings and continued,

'The peris were as pretty as motes of dust caught in a shimmering dance in a shaft of sunlight, but I was like a man possessed, for, though pretty, they did such bitter mischief. They rubbed themselves against the lips of the concubines so fiercely that the mouths of those ladies scorched. They tinkled and hung upon the ladies' nipples and milked them as if they were a herd of cows. They left little threads like snail's tracks on the velvets and brocades of the Harem's wardrobe. What was most sad to me was that those lovely girls who used to come to me for ideas for their games or arbitration in their little quarrels, now fled as soon as they saw me coming. When I did succeed in cornering a concubine, she would look back at me so big-eyed in her seeming innocence, as if I could never guess at what hanky-panky she had been getting up to with her secret little friends. Nobody was saying anything. They only wanted to be in huddles together, all giggling and smirking. Some of the girls used to smear jam on their breasts, so as to amuse themselves by trapping peris in the sticky mess. They were always asking the housekeeper for more jam. Also I recall that there was a strange new passion for cucumbers. I now know that the prick of fairy lusts led them to the cucumber, but at the time I was mightily puzzled. You will never guess how this was.'

At this point Emerald looked round the room to see if any of his audience could hazard a guess as to why the concubines should want cucumbers, but no one said anything. Perizade had been listening wide-eyed to everything Emerald was saying, but Anadil's attention was more fitful and she kept smiling at Orkhan, in such a way as to show that she did not believe a word of what they were hearing.

'Well, I will come to it presently', said Emerald. 'The little peris were skilled at archery, they carried bows strung with spiders' threads and practised on the bellies of the concubines. Then, when they were tired of archery, they would hold miniature orgies also on the bellies of the concubines. The peris would act out acrobatic sexual scenes for the young women and rehearse the same obscenities again and again, until the foul sequence of acts was known by heart. The girls on whose bodies the peris performed would pant and blush and sweetly moan at the delight of it all.'

'The Sultan was also afflicted, though differently. I sometimes took it upon myself to watch over him at nights as he slept. Then, usually in the grey hours of the dawn, my wake would be rewarded. Half dozing, I would hear the tell-tale thin, tintinnabulation and, coming close to the bed and squinting, I would observe the peris sitting on the Sultan's prick. Some would be embracing it, while others would be hammering on it with their tiny fists and imploring it to rise. Then, as it would begin to extend and rise, the peris all struggled to hang on like mad. Usually they would all be thrown off, but occasionally one of them, stronger and more determined than the others, would be triumphantly carried up on the knob of the rampant prick. Then all the others who had been thrown off would caper about it and hug its base and tickle the Sultan's balls. Finally, they would stand about waiting to be showered in the foaming white stuff and their tinkling glee would be louder than ever. In the daylight too my Sultan was plagued by these little folk. I would often see the Queen of the peris in a miniature skirt of green performing a high-kicking dance on the bridge of the Sultan's nose. He would be looking at this phantasm of delight cross-eyed and moistly drooling with lust. His prick would have shot up like a giant toadstool and he would be mad to do the impossible and get it inside her, but that was an impossible liaison. And she was sad too. They all were. The peris all wanted to have inter-course with ordinary mortals. In the end, his heart would come into his hand and they both had to be content with that. As I looked on the Sultan slump-ing back all pale and exhausted, I would hear their tinny giggling and I thought to myself ... '

Emerald puffed again at the hookah. His hands ran up and down its mouthpiece as if it were a flute. Anadil now diffidently raised a hand,

'Emerald, dearest Emerald, it is time for us to be making our way to the hammam, for Orkhan must be washed and massaged before his meeting with the Valide Sultan and his introduction to the Rapturous Chamber.'

'But I want to know what happened to the peris!' wailed Perizade. 'Where are they now?'

'Too hear is to obey,' said Emerald, 'I will escort you to the hammam and, as we walk, I will tell you how it all fell out. But, first the Sultan might like to see me make water?' He roared with laughter.

Orkhan required some urging before he could be

got to follow the eunuch into a little cubicle off the reception room. Emerald stood over the hole in the floor and reached up for a silver tube which he kept embedded in the folds of his turban. Then he pulled apart his gown and inserted the silver tube into a curiously fashioned device of ivory which seemed to be embedded in his groin. When he turned the ivory spigot, a stream of golden liquid spurted out of the silver tube. He laughed at Orkhan's surprise.

A few minutes later, they set out for the hammam down a long corridor of lotus columned arches. Now they were escorted not just by Emerald, but also by a pair of deaf mutes. From time to time, Orkhan fell back a little, so that he could admire Perizade from behind and watch the rise and fall of her large bottom. As it moved under her shiny, tight dress, he imagined that he could hear it hissing. He thought of her initial reluctance to submit to him in the pavilion and of her final hug. She appeared to pay him no attention.

After they and their escort had gone only a little way, Emerald resumed talking about the great days of the peris.

'I recall that they loved the warmth of the bathhouse. Even more, they liked to hide in lavatories. They were like cockroaches in this preference and, indeed, I often observed them fighting for the territory and using their bows and arrows to drive off the fierce insects. The peris liked to come upon a lady when she was crouching to urinate and then they would scamper under her thighs, so as to shower in the golden rain. I often watched them doing

101

this. They were endlessly fascinated by the most private functions of female bodies, they loved intimate
smells and they would spend hours carousing in the
Tavern of the Perfume-Makers. In those days (this
was in the days when Nargis was chief concubine,
before your mother, the revered Sultan Valide, sent
her the venomous hat) in those days there was a
passion among the concubines for satin knickers
trimmed with lacy frills, silk petticoats and silk
stockings with garters. Such was the fashion that
every concubine seemed to float on her own cloud of
pink or yellow frothy foam. I believe that the peris
were behind this fashion, for they loved this kind of
gossamer-delicate and intricate wear. They would
clamber into the stocking tops of the concubines and
ride about in this manner. They used to tiptoe into
the girls' knickers and snuggle there for warmth and
soft comfort . . . and, of course, the girls liked them
being there for they would receive feathery tickles
from the little creatures nestling in their underwear.
There was also a fashion for an infidel contrivance
called the bodice which held the breasts erect and
firm. Every concubine was mad to squeeze her
breasts into such a garment and the peris would follow the breasts. Then, harnessed by these dainty
things, the peris would take their ease under the soft
paps of their chosen girl.'

'Once, being curious to know what pleasure the
concubines derived from all this, I seized a pair of
Nargis's knickers. They were pink and silky and the
inside swarmed with frolicking peris. Having taken
them off Nargis, I wriggled into the knickers myself,

so as to expose my groin and bottom to the peris' delicate attentions. When I looked in the mirror, I could see them rippling under the silk and, when I looked at Nargis's face, I could see that she could see them too. However, since I was a clean-cut eunuch, there was nothing for the peris to get a hold on and, as for having a peri up the arse, I did not enjoy it. So, the peris having failed to enchant my lower parts, I was no wiser than before concerning the subtle congress between my concubines and those fairy folk. Oh, it used to drive me mad to hear the faint rustling of the peris in the silken underwear sported by the Harem! So then I and the Keeper of Lingerie used to hold regular knicker inspections and any garments that I judged unsatisfactory had to be sent to the laundry, for the peris could not stand soap. The concubines hated me for that. Even so, it was no use, for the peris were cunning at concealing themselves in the gussets and the lacy trimmings of the girl's underwear. In the end, I had to give orders that there should be no more wearing of underwear in the Harem. For, after all, no one really needs underwear. It just slows things down. And from that day to this there is no wearing of underwear in the Imperial Harem and we are all much better for that!'

'And the post of Keeper of Lingerie was abolished!' cried Perizade. 'I should have liked that rank.'

'Why are you telling us this story?' Orkhan wanted to know.

'Why! For no purpose at all, save my pleasure in the stringing of words together and in the telling of it. Must everything have a purpose?'

103

And Emerald shot Orkhan a look that seemed full of meaning, even if it was not possible to decipher what that meaning was. He continued,

'However, I was still a troubled man,' he continued. 'For the peris did not disappear with the underwear and I found that I could still hear them tinkling under the skirts of the concubines. Oh it is a subtle and sinister sensation, to hear the sound of fairy bells from under a woman's skirts! On investigating further, I found that the peris were still clambering up into the skirts and sheltering in the warmth and intimacy there afforded and the mad things used to hang on to the pubic hairs of the women and, from that safe refuge, they used to bait me by swinging and ringing their tiny bells. The madness of the bells! Those bells were driving me crazy! I tried getting the girls to lift their skirts, so that I could dust down the insides of their thighs with my hands, but really they were so disagreeable about this and, besides, there was more work in this respect than I could handle. So then I gave orders that, from that day on, all the concubines should shave their pubic hairs and that practice too has continued from that day to this. Now I was even more out of favour with the young ladies of the Harem, which saddened me, but I did it out of love for them and their innocence. And consider that one concubine had gone blind from playing with the peris!'

'However, to continue, despite having got rid of underwear and pubic hair, I remained a troubled man, for the numbers of the peris did not diminish. Indeed, I thought that I could detect new faces in their wild rout. It puzzled me how they were getting into the Harem. Then I thought about the young concubines and their passion for cucumbers, which I remembered seemed to have started at about the same time as the Harem became infested with peris. Now, the cucumber I have always thought is a rather dull vegetable. It has very little flavour. Is that not so? It is pale and watery with just a taint of bitterness. Therefore I was suspicious of the passion of the young ladies for this dull-seeming vegetable and once again I was right to be so.'

Emerald paused to ensure he had his hearers' full attention.

'The next time a consignment of cucumbers was delivered into the Harem, I pounced on them and took them into my rooms where you have been, and, on cutting a cucumber in half with my scimitar, I discovered that its centre had indeed been hollowed out and there, in the hollow, lay a sleeping peri. I brought my scimitar down once more and cut her and her vegetable chamber into tiny pieces. The next cucumber was the same. Each and every one had been cunningly hollowed out so that it could serve as a comfortable chamber for the peri who was in this manner smuggled into the Harem. So I started to work through the rest of the cucumbers with my sword, until the floor of my little room was awash with little bits of cucumber and severed limbs of peris. I gave orders that, from then on, cucumber would only be allowed into the Harem after having been thoroughly diced first. There was then naturally a problem with – '

105

Emerald broke off in mid-sentence. His eyes grew wide and he shot out an arm and pointed with a trembling finger.

'A peri! I see a peri! In that drain over there – the one that is blocked with leaves. If you hurry, you may catch it, but I believe the little creature must be trapped in the drain.'

Anadil and Perizade hurried over to the drain. Orkhan would have followed them, but Emerald seized him by the arm.

'Why am I telling you the story of my long struggle with the peris? For the mere pleasure of telling stories? I think not. Everyone knows that nothing is more important for a story than that it should have an uplifting moral. A story must have a message and the message of my story was destined for your ears alone . . . for I see you walking so docilely between those two women, following wherever Anadil takes you, as if you were a little lamb that she had on a lead. Beware of going where Anadil wants to take you! It does not have to be like that. I told my story in order to show you that anyone can take their destiny into their hands. When I was young, I kept suffering the pangs of lust for women. But I did something about it and arranged to have my prick and balls cut off. My problem was solved. When I discovered that the Harem was crawling with peris, did I lie down and let them crawl all over me too? I did not! And when I found that underwear was a problem, did I let the concubines have their way with these garments? I did not! I tugged the knickers off their bodies and made a great bonfire. I recall that the little wisps of silk carried up tongues of flame to float in the air, before descending as black rain ... And when I discovered that the peris were being smuggled into the Harem in cucumbers, did I just wave the vegetables by? Indeed no! I took a scimitar to the problem.' Emerald raised a declamatory finger. 'The message of everything that I have been telling you is obvious. Be a man!'

'I know where I am going,' said Orkhan.

'I hope so,' said Emerald.

The two women rejoined them. Perizade looked disappointed, Anadil looked doubtful.

'You found nothing?' asked Emerald. 'My mind and my eyes must have been wandering. It must have been the shadow of a leaf. It could not have been a peri, for there are no peris in the Harem any longer. I will tell you how that is.'

And he resumed his story.

'Although I now ceased to see new peris about the place, that still left hundreds of the little folk already in the Harem. What was to be done about them? I went to the Harem's library and there I consulted *The Perfumed Battlefield* and the chapter on 'The Sexual Uses of Domestic Pets'. Having done so, I sent the Agha of the Janissaries to the Animal Market and he came back with three fine Persian cats. I set these cats to hunting peris. Ah, those cats certainly loved their work! I would be sitting quietly in my room with a cat on my lap and not a peri to be seen or heard, as far as I was concerned, but then I would feel and see the cat crouching low on my lap with its spine arching and rippling and it ears pressed back. A moment later, it would shoot off me in pursuit of the invisible peri. They were great hunters those cats and good against cockroaches too. The coming of the cats inaugurated a miniature bloodbath, as a tiny war was fought out in the runnels of gutters and on the tops of wardrobes. The peris had no chance. Early on they tried to charm the cats by playing with their sexual organs, but the cats would lazily let them do that and then, just as lazily, chew them up and so the cats grew fat on fairy meat. As the numbers of the peris diminished, so the concubines grew fatter too. They were sleeping better at night and rosy tints returned to their cheeks.'

'I believe that I was present at the death of the last peri. The Queen of the peris was stronger and more cunning than most of her subjects and she had hitherto escaped the murderous cats. Azrael and I came across her in one of the flower beds that runs along the edge of the hammam. This Azrael was a rare blue Persian and the grandfather of the cat you saw in my room and he was the best of the hunters – indeed the Angel of Death. I saw the reflection of the peri Queen, sheltering under a rose petal, in the dilation of Azrael's pupils before I actually saw her running amongst the shrubs and then trying to shin up the wall of the hammam, clinging to its rough surface like a lizard. Azrael had pounced and missed twice on the ground, for she was as fast as mercury, but, once she started climbing, she slowed somewhat and that was her doom. The cat swiped at her with his paw, caught her and played with her a bit, before eating her.'

'With the peris gone, I was calm once more. The concubines pined somewhat for their vanished little friends and they hated the cats at first, but in time they came to love them – exceedingly so. Things returned to normal in the Harem and it was like a fever that had passed. But you know the saying, 'Three things are insatiable: the desert, the grave and a woman's vulva'. The next thing was that I started hearing strange talk about prayer-cushions.'

Emerald paused at a door.

'Let us go in here. I have something to show you.'

'Emerald, we should hurry on to the hammam.'

'This will only take a moment,' he replied reassuringly. 'It is something to see.'

They followed the eunuch into a lumber room, full of discarded objects of pleasure – a couple of unstrung dulcimers, some archery quivers whose stitching had come loose, a leather mattress, some boxes of white crystals, the effigy of a woman stuffed with straw. Orkhan had briefly fantasised that the eunuch had brought them there to show them a prayer-cushion, but, no, Emerald brought them over to a table on which there was a model of a building – or rather of a group of buildings.

'I confiscated it from the concubines,' said Emerald.

Looking closer Orkhan saw that it was a miniature, wooden replica of the Harem. First, he found the Cage and the Passage Where the Jinns Consult. Then, having got his bearings, he found the porcelain pavilion, the chamber of the ice-pit and the zoo.

'They had made it from thousands of toothpicks, in order to house their peris,' claimed Emerald.

Anadil looked doubtful.

'They were going to lodge their favourite peris in these tiny buildings and play harems with them. But I brought in the cats, before its building was quite finished.' Emerald sighed. 'The peris used to piss in my eyes at night as I slept, so that I could hardly get the lids apart in the morning and I hated them as much as they hated me. Still it makes me sad to see this fine building so abandoned. I do believe that the girls were going to imprison some of the peris in these toy buildings and keep them there so that they forgot everything about the outside world. I think they were even going to use delicate little needles to make a few of the peris into eunuchs. I should like to have seen that. . . .'

Back in the corridor, Orkhan heard Anadil whispering to Perizade,

'Emerald's stories are ridiculous. Still, he is a great lover . . . even though the business with the chocolates is a bit messy.'

The eunuch's former sunniness had by now quite vanished. He was a sombre and silent escort for the remainder of their walk to the hammam.

CHAPTER SEVEN

WATER SPORTS

A few more steps brought them to the Imperial Laundry. Perizade went in to find Orkhan a clean robe. He caught a glimpse of vast vats and mangles and of hefty women using great wooden paddles to stir the vats. There was a stale reek of damp clothes. When Perizade re-emerged with the robe, Anadil said,

'Say goodbye to Perizade. She has to go back to her work now.'

But Orkhan took her in his arms,

'Do not leave me, Perizade. I need you.'

And, blushing, she whispered back,

'I know that I am queen of your heart, for it is written on the folds of my cunt.'

And they kissed.

Anadil was furious,

'You have to come with me! The ladies of the Harem are waiting for you. Go back to work, Perizade!' And, as Perizade reluctantly re-entered the laundry, Anadil continued, 'Perizade is too stupid to understand our mysteries. That is why she is a washerwoman and not a concubine. Now, it is time to clean you up.'

The laundry and the hammam were next door to one another, for they both drew on the same system of hot-water pipes. The approach to the hammam was lined by a corps of eunuchs bearing scimitars.

'It is time you were washed and perfumed. We cannot let your mother see you looking like this.'

Emerald and the deaf mutes joined the other guards at the door of the hammam, as if the place was about to become Orkhan's prison. Anadil took him by the hand and together they descended into the changing room. First Anadil undressed Orkhan. He hated to see how his cock stiffened in response to her delicate fingers, for by now he knew that he detested Anadil. And, as she looked into his eyes, it was clear that she knew it too, but she licked her lips and turned to press her flank against his groin, before asking him to unhook her dress.

A little black girl entered and served them wine. Anadil drew Orkhan down onto the cushions and pressed cup after cup on him, saying that he would find it easier to face what was coming if he had drunk a little.

'First there will be an opportunity to practise the Dolorous Gaze on ordinary girls,' she said. 'You may look, but not touch, for in that way your desire will be intensified. We need to intensify your desire. Have some more wine and watch me.'

Like a serpent uncoiling, she rose from the cushions and began to dance. He heard the slap of her feet on the stone and the jangle of her anklets as she moved, but she seemed to dance to a music that was inaudible to ordinary mortals. Orkhan thought with regret of Perizade. He now knew that he hated Anadil, yet at the same time, as he watched Anadil dance, he was aware that she had drawn him into her thrall once more. Swivel-hipped, she came up close and stood over him and thrust her belly at his face and made its muscles roll and ripple. She turned and shook her bottom, so that its flesh seemed to shimmer before his eyes. Then she retreated and, with her head at an angle, she undulated and arched her back and rose on her toes, as if she were making love standing up to a creature made of air. She was glowing and sweating gently and her face was soft and dreamy. Then she seemed to remember Orkhan and moved in a serpentine glide towards him once more and drew her hands up over her thighs and hips. He thought that he might choke in the clouds of her bitter perfume.

'I want to hear that you worship me,' she said. 'I want to hear that you will do anything I ask of you.'

Orkhan was trembling. Simultaneously, crazed and sane, he knew that some mad thing must follow her request, but at the same time, he knew that his lust for her was such that there was no power in him to refuse her anything she might ask for.

He threw himself forward to kiss her feet and, having done so, heard himself saying,

'I worship you, Anadil. I am your slave and will do anything you require of me.'

Anadil had her hands on her hips. She had been dancing as if her life had depended on it, but now she looked coolly down on him and replied,

'But I remember that only yesterday you were ready to have me executed. Now you have learnt something, have you not? You want me so much . . . As I stand here, I could urinate all over you. Would you dare stop me?'

115

'If my mistress pleases . . . '

'Well as it happens, I prefer to urinate in private and I am not accustomed to pee over men. Orkhan, my business with you is all but finished. I will kiss you once more, but that will only be when you are dead. Now pick up my clothes and deliver them to one of the slaves outside, so that they can be taken off to the laundry. Then it is time for you to be washed, perfumed and massaged.'

Orkhan did as he was told. Then she took him by the hand and led him through a series of small cells, flagged and furnished in marble. The wet floors were treacherous underfoot. They passed through a slightly larger room, a tepidarium, where a couple of women lay on stone slabs sweating into their towels and from there they passed into the calidarium.

By now Orkhan was beyond surprise. The calidarium was vast and sulphorous and shafts of sunlight from the leaded widows in the roof streamed down between the clouds of steam and incense which rose from the water. Orkhan had never seen so much water before. The place was full of naked women who appeared and disappeared in those clouds. A few of the women splashed about in the water or sported round the central fountain which was fashioned in the form of a trio of entwined serpents. Another gang of women were running a race around the pool's edge, their breasts flapping wildly as they ran. Others at the far end of the calidarium were dancing and singing as they danced. These women paid no attention to Orkhan and Anadil, but others seated and sprawled around the edge of the calidarium turned to look at them as they entered. Some hunched over the incense braziers, drinking wine or braiding each other's hair. Bowls of cucumbers and hard-boiled eggs had been placed here and there throughout the hammam and some women picnicked on these. A couple of elderly concubines smoked long chibouk pipes. One was at work with a depilatory brush. So many naked bodies, running, sitting, lying, fondling, squatting, standing, bending, caressing, writhing, imploring – it ought to have been Paradise, yet to Orkhan, who longed to escape from it, it was more like a vision of the Last Judgement.

Then in between the surges of the women's singing, Orkhan heard a man's voice,

'I would not say that my wife is ugly but . . . '

It was the Vizier. Like everyone else he was naked. He stood near the edge of the pool, surrounded by a group of young concubines and he was juggling eggs and cucumbers as he continued to describe his wife.

'. . . but she is an acceptable substitute for masturbation, if I concentrate and use my imagination.'

'What is the Vizier doing here?'

'Oh Orkhan, don't be such a bore. Surely you must have guessed by now? He's not the real Vizier. The real Vizier would never be allowed to set foot in the Harem. That little man is just one of the Harem's buffoons. We appointed him to play the Vizier. He is, like most of what you have encountered, just part of our charade.'

Anadil summoned over a dark-skinned young woman.

117

'This is Afsana. She invents the stories for us to play out. She gives us our roles and makes sure we know our lines.'

Afsana looked modestly down.

Anadil continued,

'It would be so boring otherwise, just sitting around in the Harem, waiting for a man to appear. We all take turns at playing the different parts. Otherwise, even the masquerade would get dull. But now the time for games is almost over,' concluded Anadil regretfully.

'So the Prayer-Cushion cult is all just a game you have invented to while away your captivity?'

Anadil looked shocked,

'Holy Mother, no! No, the way of the Prayer-Cushion is sacred truth. All our masques and games are part of our service as Prayer-Cushions – part of our the quest for the Holy Rapture and an expression of our desire to serve you.'

Anadil might have said more, but at that moment, three young concubines, who had been running round the edge of the pool, came trotting up to Orkhan.

'Would you like to race with us?' asked the first concubine breathlessly. 'My name is Gulanar.'

'And I am Najma.'

'And I Parvana.'

They crowded round Orkhan.

'If you catch one of us, you can do with her as you please,' said Najma.

'I can do with you as I please already,' said Orkhan.

'Well, you will have to catch us first,' said Parvana and with that she tweaked at his penis. At that same moment, Najma pulled his nose and Gulanar slapped at his bottom. Then they turned and, like startled deer, broke into a run. Without thinking, Orkhan started to run after them. The marble floor was hot and slippery and he was somewhat drunk. The shrieks of the other concubines who sat and watched the runners echoed and re-echoed in the muffled acoustics of the hammam. As Parvana, who led the running concubines, pushed past the Vizier, the circle of boiled eggs and cucumbers that the latter had been keeping going in the air fell to the ground and were trampled underfoot.

Gulanar was an ungainly runner and soon fell behind the others and, when she looked back, this slowed her yet further. Orkhan was almost upon her and ready to lunge and catch at her waist when, with a squeal of alarm, she leapt sideways and hurled herself into the water. Najma and Parvana now stopped running and waited until Orkhan was almost upon them before following Gulanar into the pool. The breasts of the trio of concubines seemed to float on the water and the sunlight rippled over their bodies in quavering patterns. They splashed up at Orkhan.

'You have not caught us yet!' taunted Najma. 'You will have to join us in the water.

'Please come and play with us here,' added Gulanar.

And then the three maidens began to sing a strange, senseless song of enchantment,

119

'Wagala Weia! Wagala, weiala weia!
Wallala! Wallala! Heia! Ha ha!'

As they sang, they swam towards the pool's edge where Orkhan was standing.

'It is better under water,' said Parvana and she pulled at Orkhan's ankles so that he toppled in.

They swam around him, splashing water in his face. They were laughing at him, but he stood terrified and hesitating, for he had never been in a pool of water before. Their soft bellies and thighs trembled in the water's movement. He made a lunge for Najma. She dived below the surface and, after hesitating an instant, he followed. He had his hands around her hips, but then he was being pulled back by one of the other concubines, and eel-like Najma slithered free of his embrace. Orkhan turned to confront Gulanar who continued to undulate seductively beneath the surface and baited him with her breasts. He waded towards her and then plunged beneath the surface. He felt something nip at his inner thigh. It was Parvana who nibbled at the insides of his legs with her teeth. He was about to turn on her when a pair of hands closed over his eyes. He had to break free and surface for air.

Gulanar stood a few feet away from him,

'Over here my lover! Over here!' I can give you what you want, but, as he waded towards her, she slipped under the surface and skimmed away.

'Choose me! I am prettier than her,' sang out Parvana now behind him.

And so it continued. At last, Orkhan confessed

himself defeated and pulled himself out of the pool
and he lay on its edge, finding it difficult to get his
breath back in the sulphur-laden air. With a start, he
saw reflected in the water what he took to be a white
spectre hunched behind him on the edge of the pool.
Among so many naked women, this figure shrouded
in damp, clinging white cloths seemed like an
annunciation of death.

Turning round, he saw that Anadil had arrived to
stand beside the spectral figure.

'Surely you recognise Mihrimah?' asked Anadil.
'However much she covers herself up, her shape gives
her away. But I am afraid her arrival signals that our
time for games is almost over. It only remains for us
to massage and perfume you in preparation for the
final ritual.'

Then sensing Orkhan's apprehension and hostility,
she continued,

'I know that these last two days have been hard for
you. But all your ordeals are going to end very soon.
Trust me. Trust us. It is very important for you to
be relaxed now. That is why we are going to massage
you.'

And Anadil and Mihrimah led him to a large stone
slab set on brass feet, surrounded by braziers of
burning spikenard. They began with him lying on his
front, while she walked up and down his back, dig-
ging her toes into his back as she did so. He felt his
body buckle and slowly soften under her feet. By the
time she had finished this exercise and clambered
down, Parvana, Najma and Gulanar had clustered
round the slab and together the four of them set to

121

pummelling and kneading the body of Orkhan with their hands. Mihrimah stood looking on. Anadil, as she worked, kept whispering to Orkhan about how important it was that he relax himself utterly, that he feel himself to be soft and weak.

'For the seducer always seduces from a position of weakness.'

The concubines rolled him over and the fingers of the women moved inexorably towards his groin, probing and exploring. His testicles were gently squeezed by Parvana while Anadil anointed his penis with a yellowish unguent. He entertained the fantasy that he was floating in the air, his body being kept up by thousands of tiny butterflies trapped inside him, which flapped and beat their wings.

Finally Mihrimah raised her wide sleeved arms, so that she looked like a great white cormorant about to fly. It was a signal that the massage could be prolonged no further.

'There is just barely time to show you the Rapturous Chamber,' said Anadil. 'It will be best if you see it first, for the unknown is always so frightening, is it not? But if you have seen the place, it will be easier for you to envisage what is going to happen in it.'

Orkhan walked shakily between Anadil and Mihrimah back into the tepidarium. Here he was handed a plain white cotton robe which he slipped on. Then from the tepidarium they passed through a door he had not noticed before into a reception chamber, and without pausing, the three of them entered the Rapturous Chamber.

The walls and vaulted ceiling of the Rapturous Chamber were covered in mirror-mosaic, whose glass fragments were framed in intricate tendrils of silver arabesque. Hundreds of candles burned and glittered in niches set into the walls. The floor was surfaced in porphyry. Most of the surface, however, was occupied by a great pool of quicksilver on which floated an inflated mattress, covered in silk and tethered at its corners by silken cords. So silver burned on silver and it was some moments before Orkhan, dazzled, realised that a woman stood at the far end of the quicksilver pool. The woman wore a plumed turban and was sheathed in a tight silver dress whose long train fanned out over the porphyry. The woman, seeing Orkhan stare at her, made an exultant gesture with her raised and clenched fist.

It was Roxelana. Orkhan turned to Anadil.

'Oh Orkhan! How can you be so boring and stupid?' Anadil was pouting in exasperation. 'Of course it is Roxelana. It just happened to be her turn to play the animal girl. We all take turns at the different parts. Sometimes I am the one who laughs; sometimes I am the one who sheds tears. Otherwise it would be too boring . . . though it is true that Babur seems to like Roxelana best. She, like the rest of us, is a masquerader – part of the Harem's spiritual theatre. As a Prayer-Cushion, however, she is on a lower level than Mihrimah, so, after you failed your night of vigil with Mihrimah, we realised that you could not have been ready for such an exalted sexual experience and we chose Roxelana to take you through something lower and more physical. It was

123

my fault. I thought that you might have been ready for Mihrimah, when clearly you were not. Still Roxelana probably gave you what you needed . . . '

She looked as though she was going to say a lot more, but at that moment a ragged fanfare of shawms accompanied by cymbals sounded outside the Rapturous Chamber.

'The Valide Sultan has arrived,' said Anadil, looking apprehensive. 'I only hope we are not approaching the final ritual performance too quickly.'

CHAPTER EIGHT

DYING OF PLEASURE

When Orkhan in the Cage had fantasised about life outside its walls, he had had no idea that the reality would be so strange. Together with Anadil, he passed through the outer reception room and emerged into daylight once more. The Valide Sultan, dressed in heavy black and red brocade and flanked by attendant concubines and eunuchs, stood waiting on the grass. This was the first time that Orkhan had seen her when she was not laughing. She stepped forward to brush at his hair with an anxious gesture. Then she embraced him, before pulling back a little, so that her hands rested on his shoulders, and she began to address him,

'Beloved son, this is your mother's proudest day of her life. Beloved son, you are now only a few moments away from encountering your betrothed and consummating the marriage which for so many years I have been dreaming of for a child of mine.'

Although the Valide Sultan faced Orkhan directly, she did not seem to see him. She was gazing into the past, staring at it with such intensity that she seemed to see everything that had vanished so many years ago in perfect detail.

'I was born in the Harem,' she continued. 'And I have spent all my life within its walls. I remember that, when I was little, I had a toy model of the Harem, perfect in every detail, to play with. I used to put my dolls in it and have them play at harems, for of course I knew of no other world. I used to arrange weddings and wedding-feasts for my dolls within its tiny rooms. But there was one particular doll, which was an especial favourite of mine, whom I could not marry off for a long time. This was because I could not think of a bride who should be noble enough, rich enough and beautiful enough to become the wife of my favourite doll. Then one day I was inspired and decided that he could marry the Divinity and then there could be the grandest of all wedding feasts for such a mystic marriage.'

She sighed, reluctant to leave her memories,

'That was long ago and all in play. Yet what the child dreamed of in play has come to fruit in reality today. For Orkhan, beloved son of mine, I have betrothed you to the Divinity. Even now the Goddess is hastening to your bed. Listen!'

Orkhan, listening, heard nothing save his mother's stertorous breathing.

'She is close! Very close!' the Valide Sultan insisted. 'Just now She is like a gentle breeze stirring in the tops of the trees. Then, when She comes to you, She will be like a forest fire and, finally, when you consummate your love you will be swept up in the flaming cyclone of Her embrace – or so it may seem to you. But who can describe congress with the Infinite? Here I am, an ordinary mortal, and I am trying to tell you in words about something for which there can be no words.'

Now the Valide Sultan really did look at Orkhan and her voice hardened,

'I see from your eyes that you are afraid. Do not be so. You are only a day out of the Cage and you have already enjoyed several women. Yet the delights you have experienced with them will come to seem as nothing when the Goddess comes to your bed. You will look back on your first fumbling explorations of sex with women and, by comparison with what you have since experienced, it will seem to you that you were then fucking creatures no more substantial than shadows. Foolish people think that the ultimate mystery of life resides in the spirit. The wise know that it is found nowhere save in the flesh. The Goddess who is even now beginning to spread Her mighty thighs is the fleshly incarnation of ultimate love and all other women are merely the ghostly and reflected images of Her infinitely voluptuous body. She is robed in oceans and sunsets. But she will strip herself for you. Do you not like the firm breasts of young women? The Goddess has breasts which are larger than mountains.'

'I will try to describe the fierce delight of being in bed with her. Your hair will stand on end and your eyeballs will pop out of their sockets and you will bite your tongue and she will crack your spine in her embrace and that will only be the beginning of it. Death is the bed on which the lover joins the Beloved. Yet, I promise you, you will not want to resist, for She will seem to you dearer than life itself, and you will yearn only to be melted in Her flames. As you melt with desire, you will experience yourself in a state of liquefaction and it will seem to you that your whole body is being melted into semen, until you are ejaculated out of your own penis in a paradox of ecstasy. Orgasm comes as a flash of white lightning filling the dark horizon of the soul. In a single love-bite the Goddess will devour you, so that you are She and She you, so that you will find yourself shafting yourself.'

The Valide Sultan paused, lost in this vision, before resuming in a steadier voice,

'After you have been bedded by the Goddess, you will see Her in all other women and experience infinite rapture with them as often as you choose. This is what it means to become the Golden Man and it will be proved when you take Mihrimah to bed, for, after you have been bedded by the Goddess, then straightaway you will take Mihrimah as your second wife and embrace her, and it may be that with the Goddess's favour Mihrimah will conceive. In such a manner, I shall become the grandmother of a child of the Divinity, something which I have yearned for since girlhood.'

'Mother, I am not ready for this honour. I think that I need more time for preparation. I should like some time to think about my duties as a bridegroom.'

She smiled reassuringly,

'I only wish I was a man so that I could take the Goddess to bed. If only I could make you understand how it will be, then you would certainly not still be standing here talking to an old woman like me, for you would be rushing to the bridal chamber, anxious not to delay your meeting with the Beloved by a single minute. You are young and healthy and Anadil, Mihrimah and Roxelana are all good girls. They are appointed handmaidens of the Goddess and they have made you as ready as you will ever be. I know that you are not going to disappoint me, as Barak did. The Goddess made the world in order to be loved by it, so you cannot help but love her when she comes for you. But I should not stand here prattling away like someone who has lost her wits. I will leave Mihrimah here to describe the precise manner of your love-making with the Divinity and what you must do to please your bride. I will now hurry away to the Porcelain Pavilion, where my girls are even now preparing a post-nuptial feast. Beloved son, I will be waiting for you there and anxiously hoping to hear of your emergence from the Chamber of Rapture.'

With that she abruptly kissed Orkhan on the brow and walked away.

Now Mihrimah and Anadil came close to him and Mihrimah began to speak in a low muffled voice,

'Now you know that your mother glories in the fact that it is one of her sons who is about to become the Golden Man. It now falls upon me to explain the sequence of actions to be followed when we return to the Rapturous Chamber.'

She paused to check that she had all his attention, before insisting,

'It is most important that you should be fully aware of what you are about to undergo.'

'It is better to know what is going to happen,' chimed in Anadil, 'for the unknown is always frightening, is it not?'

131

And Mihrimah resumed her speech,

'This is how it will happen. There will be just the four of us – you, me, Anadil and, of course, Roxelana, for she is one of the strongest of the concubines. Together we four will enter the Rapturous Chamber. We will undress you, and you will assist in my undressing. Next, as you stand in contemplation of me in my lustrous nakedness, Anadil will take your cock in her mouth. Then swiftly – it must be very swift – Roxelana will produce the silken bowstring and throttle you. You will then ejaculate in the ecstasy of the Death of the Just Man and, in so doing, experience the Holy Rapture, which is the gift of the Goddess. Yet you will be dead for an instant only, for Anadil will have collected in her mouth all your semen, which contains the departing life force, and she will swiftly deliver your semen back to you in a loving kiss. Now the dead man drinks of the dead man's seed and chokes and shudders back into life once more. Thus you will be awakened by the Kiss of Death and so resurrected to a state of perpetual bliss, as the Holy Rapture fills every particle of your body for ever and ever. You will not be as before, for you will have become the Golden Man and the Goddess will dwell within your body and you two will be joined together in a state of perpetual orgasm. Having died and been reborn, you will come to me on the Bed of Rapture which floats on the silver pool and, as you embrace me, I too shall be swept up in ecstasy and I will take your seed in my womb. It is all a tremendous and marvellous mystery.'

Then, seeing the expression on Orkhan's face, she continued,

'Do not worry. We know what to do. It is all in *The Perfumed Battlefield*, in the last chapter which is entitled "How to Give Ultimate Pleasure to your Man".'

Anadil interrupted,

'It is true that things went wrong with Barak, but that was because he lost his nerve at the last moment and struggled, so that I could not keep my mouth round his cock, and thus his seed was wasted on the floor. But, if you do not struggle, all shall be well. You have had enough wine though. I think I gave you just the right amount to drink and you should be relaxed.'

'You have to lose yourself completely to find yourself, according to *The Perfumed Battlefield*,' Mihrimah continued. 'If our earlier charades have had any purpose, other than beguilement, it was to teach that the one who loses wins and that the one who wins loses. It is always like that in the warfare between the sexes.'

'Well, I do not really understand such matters,' replied Orkhan. 'But I have had enough of talk and I see no path open to me, save the one which leads to the Rapturous Chamber. I suppose the sooner that I reach my predestined end the better it will be for me.'

Hearing this, Mihrimah raised her arms and the concubines and eunuchs who stood outside the hammam began to sing a strange song, which began with the words 'I have drunk the waters of the Beloved and She has drunk from mine.'

Emerald pointed back to the door of the hammam and Orkhan began to walk towards it. As he did so, concubine after concubine threw herself in front of him, so that he trod upon the spines of Gulanar, Najma, Parvana and others whose names he did not know. He was walking upon a carpet of human flesh. Nevertheless, Orkhan did not glance at the backs of the women he trod upon but instead looked up at the sky overhead.

Passing through the ante-room, Orkhan led them back into the Rapturous Chamber. Anadil and Roxelana stripped him of his white robe and tossed it into the pool. It rested on the bubbling surface a few moments, before abruptly vanishing. Multiple reflections of gold and silver on silver made Orkhan dizzy. Mihrimah waited on the far side of the pool, until he was ready to assist in her undressing. His fingers trembled as he set to work removing the layers of cloth and she had to tell him not to be in such a hurry.

She smiled at what she took to be his lustful impatience,

'In desiring my body, you have learned to love the transient and that is a good and necessary stage. But it is a stage that you must pass beyond, for, in the end, only the Devil loves what is passing.'

Finally, Mihrimah's white robe, veil and shawl lay at her ankles and she stood naked and very beautiful. However, he was not suffered to linger at her side. Anadil beckoned him back to the other side of the pool. Beside her stood Roxelana, resplendent in her silver dress. In one hand Roxelana held up the train of the dress, in the other she dangled the silken bowstring.

'Turn to face Mihrimah,' she said as Orkhan walked towards her.

He did so and Anadil knelt in front of him and reached for his cock, which fear had made small and soft.

'Do not worry,' said Anadil. 'It becomes hard in an instant.'

And she pressed her lips to it.

'Look to the lustrous Mihrimah,' said Roxelana, who now stood directly behind him.

Mihrimah stood at the far end of the chamber, radiant and glorying in her nakedness.

Orkhan sensed rather than saw Roxelana stretching to raise the silken bowstring above his head. She began to speak,

'In the name of the Holy Rapture – '

As the cord came over his head, Orkhan reached for it and pulled hard. At the same time he bent double, so that Roxelana was pulled onto his back. Then he had her by her wrists and brought her over him and down on top of the kneeling Anadil, and together the two women were sent tumbling into the quicksilver pool. Its momentarily turbulent surface closed over their heads in interlinked rippling whorls. Glittering bubbles rose and exploded.

Next Orkhan went after Mihrimah. She attempted to escape by running round the far side of the pool, but she was less agile than Parvana, Najma and Gulanar had earlier proved themselves, and Orkhan,

135

having caught her at the door, swiftly had his arms round her throat.

'Is there a way from here to the laundry?'

Her voice was wheezy in reply,

'The laundry? Yes, if you go back to the tepidarium. I think there is a passage from there to the laundry. The slaves use it to fetch fresh towels.'

'You are going to take me there.'

The handful of the women lying cooling in the tepidarium did not give them a second glance. Orkhan walked behind Mihrimah with his hands encircling her throat down the passageway which led out of the tepidarium and through a series of doors into the laundry. They entered the hall full of vats that Orkhan had previously glimpsed on his way to the hammam and, as they did so, the women who worked there started shrieking and throwing up their hands. Perizade, who seemed to be their overseer, came hurrying up to deal with this bizarre intrusion.

'Perizade, I need your help. I need you. Together we are going to try and escape from the Harem.'

'It is death to even think of such a thing,' she replied.

Even so she did not hesitate. First, she dismissed the other laundry-women from the hall of vats. Secondly, she began to tear up strips of cloth and together she and Orkhan set to gagging and tying up Mihrimah. They were not kind to her and, despite her moist, pleading eyes, their knots were tight and the cloths bit deep into her soft flesh. She was bound in such a fashion that her face was pressed down over her knees with her arms tied behind her back.

Orkhan was bent low over Mihrimah, checking the knots when he was knocked over, by a cracking blow to the side of his face. He rolled over and looked up. It was Roxelana. Her eyes glittered and her face had a curious greyish look about it. Tiny drops of silver fell from her dress with every movement.

'I now know that I was too gentle the last time,' she said. 'This time it is going to be really bloody. The jinns in me are parched for your blood. They are going to suck your soul out through your arse.'

She hitched her dress to deliver a kick, but, even so, her kick was constrained and had little force. She was panting heavily and she seemed to be having difficulty in seeing Orkhan. Nevertheless, she threw herself upon him and began to pound at him with her fists. He fought back, yet not as strongly as he should have done, for he felt himself unmanned, half-mesmerised by this strange, lead-grey creature, more demon than woman, who chanted in a strange language as she beat at his chest and face. She was trying to kill him, yet still he felt the stirring of desire and he wanted to kiss her even as they fought. Then suddenly it was as if one of the jinns in her body had made away for another. The glittering eyes softened and she fell forward on him.

'I am too weak to resist you. I want you inside me,' her voice was pleading.

Her mouth was questing for his and with one of her hands she was seeking to hoick her skirt further up.

'You want it too. Just a little soft, lingering kiss will be enough . . . '

137

She pressed her mouth hard against his.

It was Perizade who brought this perilous seduction to an end as she came up from behind and swung a laundry paddle at the back of Roxelana's head, so that the brilliant eyes went suddenly dull.

'We need her dress,' said Perizade. 'Get her dress off her.'

This was not easy, for the dress was tight and Roxelana was heavy. As they struggled with the limp body and clinging fabric, Perizade explained that though the concubines were confined to the Harem, their servants were not. The latter were often sent out into the city on errands. Orkhan's only chance of escaping the Harem alive was to be disguised as a woman in Perizade's company.

Leaving Orkhan to struggle into the dress, Perizade went off to look for shawls to cover his head and shoulders. Orkhan had managed by wriggling to get the dress half way up his hips when he heard a rasping voice behind him,

'That is my dress you have on and I want it back.'

Roxelana staggered towards him. By now her skin had turned deep black and her eyeballs seemed to have shrivelled in their sockets.

'Oh my prince!' she continued throatily. 'Just one dying kiss. That is all we need to consummate our love. Just one little kiss.'

She seemed to sniff her way towards him. She put her arms around him and stuck out her tongue. It was like a twig of charred wood. She coughed and a gob of mercury appeared on her lower lip and swiftly ran down her chin. Then she loosened her

138

clasp round Orkhan's neck and slowly sank to die at his feet.

Perizade reappeared with plain white shawls. She did not give the corpse of Roxelana so much as a glance. One shawl covered Orkhan's shoulders, the other went over his head and he held it together across his face with his teeth. Together they walked out of the laundry and they passed by the Valide Sultan, who was anxiously pacing about in the garden. They were detained for a while by the Janissary guards at the gate out of the Inner Court. Perizade explained to one of the soldiers that the furnaces which served the hammam and laundry were about to run out of firewood and that they were being sent on a mission to hurry up the next delivery.

While they waited for the young Janissary to return from consulting with his officer, Perizade turned and whispered to Orkhan,

'Why did you come to me?'

'It was as you said. We are destined to be together. I am destined to love you and I do. I need you – and, besides my viper needs to drink at your tavern. It is a hopeless addiction.'

'That viper and tavern stuff!' Perizade laughed. 'That's just Harem folklore. It is merely one of the stories made up by Afsana and the other concubines. You must just like the taste, that's all!'

The Janissary returned and indicated that they might walk on. So they passed through the Gate of the Inner Court into the Outer Court, which was open to the public. The real world of old and young men and women, children and animals, carts, traps, sacking, planks, bales, barrels, hides, bottles, lanterns and knives seemed to explode before Orkhan's eyes. He had left the tainted fairyland of silk, silver and porphyry forever.

Under assumed names, Orkhan and Perizade found work in the city. They prospered and, after only a few years, they set up a laundry of their own in the village of Eyup beyond the walls of Istanbul and there they continued to dwell in contentment until they were overtaken by Death, the breaker of bonds and destroyer of delights.